Sussex Tales

Also by Jan Edwards:

Leinster Gardens and Other Subtleties
*The Alchemy Press Book of Ancient Wonders**
*The Alchemy Press Book of Urban Mythic**
*The Alchemy Press Book of Urban Mythic 2**
*Wicked Women**
*co-edited with Jenny Barber

Sex, Lies and Family Ties (as Sarah J Graham)

The *Margrave of the South Coast*,
an urban fantasy series, begins in 2015 with
The Brighton Belles Damned

Jan Edwards in a writer of fantasy fiction with a passion for folklore, myths and legends, which she puts to use in many of her forty-published stories. She was short-listed in 2011 for the BFS Award for Best Short Story. Jan is an editor with the Alchemy Press and Fox Spirit Books. In civvy-street she has been (amongst other things) a bookseller and master locksmith but is now a Reiki master, meditational healer, Taroist and writer. She was born and raised in Sussex, though now lives in the Staffordshire Moorlands in a house with a very steep garden, three cats and her husband Peter.

janedwardsblog.wordpress.com

Sussex Tales

Jan Edwards

PENKHULL

Penkhull Press, Staffordshire, UK

www.penkhullpress.co.uk

Contents

Dedication

To Pop for being Pop.

To the Weirdoes Workshop,
where these tales began...

...and to Renegade Writers,
where they ended up.

And most of all to Peter...
...for being Peter

Prologue

The 1950s and 60s was an odd time for rural communities. The war, and its legions of Land Army girls, was gone and with mechanisation taking another giant stride forward, the old ways were all but vanished. No more horse ploughs. No more hedge laying. No more teams of workers needed for harvesting and hay making. One cowman could milk a whole herd of cows that had taken bevy of milkmaids in his father's day.

It was not merely old farming methods that were vanishing, however. The entire seasonal flow of rural life was changing forever. People were no longer fixed to the rhythms of the land and all the traditions that went with it. Harvest suppers that had once taken place on every farmstead, as the last sheaf was carried home, had dwindled to church socials. Wassailing was no longer relevant when ancient orchards were being ripped out to make more efficient and productive use of the land. And as the labour force decreased the simple hedgerow harvesting of blackberries and sloes, or Sunday assaults on rabbit warrens, decreased with them.

This book is an echo of that era. The tales included here are based on snippets gathered amongst family, friends and neighbours to reflect the world I experienced going on around me. An echo perhaps, but one I hope will always be remembered in some small way.

Birch Sap Poachers

There was a lamb in the oven. Not a joint, or a chop, or even a shepherd's pie from Sunday's leftovers. On that particular morning the Aga door was wide open, all of the shelves removed, and there, curled into an old meat tin, was a new-born lamb no bigger than the teddy bear that sat upstairs on my bed.

The tiny animal raised its head, opened its eyes, and with its head thrusting forward and its pink mouth open, trumpeted a thin, rusty wailing; full of demands and defiance and pathos all at once. It was plainly out of sorts and saw me as the possible if not probable cause.

My mother flapped her teacloth in our general direction as she bustled around in her usual breakfast-hustle. 'Feeling a bit perkier?' she said. 'Well, you wait a bit. I'll fetch you some milk for your breakfast.'

I assumed she was talking to the lamb because, despite living on a farm, she knew I did not drink milk if I could avoid it. In her book there was nothing that could not be cured with food and tea. Doling out food in prodigious quantities was her way of signalling comfort and affection.

I wasn't quite so sure when she poured cereal into a bowl, and placed it in front of me. Quite obviously both lamb and I were being tended on auto-pilot. Her attention was not fixed on food but on my father and his latest doings.

'So what happened then, Stan?' she asked.

My father laughed, slapping his calloused hands on either side of a large demijohn and making the jar's cloudy contents slop and gurgle. 'The Guv'nor wanted two brace for his dinner party come the weekend, and you know he won't go after en hisself, not out of season, not even when they're all flying over from Dranton estate. He's not above asking me to bag 'im a couple though. Anyway, I was goin' up past Tone Ley and working across to the pheasant chee, when I hears voices. So I drops down quiet like, an' creeps up, an' there was these two lads, hangin' about in the shadows.'

'Did they have guns?' Mother's tone was curt from her fear for him and I could see her point. One man with a thumb stick and a hessian bag was no match against armed poachers.

My father nodded. 'One of them,' he said. 'I'd thought as they were poachin', and maybe they were an' all. But then they stopped by that stand of birches just up the other side of the Manor road.' He paused, aware that I was listening. 'So I stayed right where I was. They didn't have a clue I was there,' he added, and shot me another reproving glance. 'Anyhow … they was fiddling around for quite a while and I couldn't make out what they were up to from that distance. Then our old dog caught up and comes straight past me, all gas and noise, hackles up, gnashers on show, an' ee took the arse straight out of the biggest one's trousers. The pair of them took off like a pair a robbutts ... and left this behind en.' He slapped the jar again and laughed. 'It's birch sap. Alby reckons it makes a good drop. Get us a pound of raisins from the Stores-van when he comes round, will you, love? An' a couple of bags of sugar. I'll get a good gallon out of this lot.'

He grinned at her and her eyes laughed back, though the rest of her face maintained its habitual pursed-lipped judgement. Many people wondered how these two ever made a pair, but I think that was it, right there. He made her laugh.

Mother sighed, eyeing him with suppressed amusement, and said. 'White or brown?'

'Whatever's cheapest, duck. It makes no odds.'

'Dad,' I said. 'If they were poachers, what was they after?' I leaned forward, eager for the details mother would never ask. 'Was it a stag, Dad? Or robbutts?'

He only laughed. 'Stag? No, poppet. Not over that stretch. Them lads might've took a pheasant or two if they got the chance.'

'So was you poachin' then, Dad?' I said.

He hesitated, glancing toward my mother. 'No ... it's on the Guv'nor's land,' he said, finally. 'So I weresn't poachin'. And don't you go tellin' all your mates at school. Especially them Garton boys.' He waved a finger at me in a half-hearted warning. 'I don't want folks knowing we've got chees in that wood or we'll have en all down here. Promise?'

I dug my spoon into my breakfast, avoiding his eye. I didn't like keeping those kinds of secrets. They were no fun. Just for once I had a genuine tale of late night skull-duggery, a real coup, and my father was expecting me to keep it to myself.

'Promise?' he said again.

I nodded as vaguely as I could get away with. Time to change the subject. 'Can I get down from the table Mum?'

'Yes. Have you brushed your teeth?'

'Yes, Mum.'

'Dinner money?'

'Yes, Mum ... is it going to be all right? I mean will it go back to it's *yowe*? Or is en goin' to be a *sock*?'

I jerked my thumb at the lamb and my mother frowned. 'No idea,' she said. 'It's such a windshaken creature.' She tapped me briskly on the arm. 'Duffel-bag. Now. Come on. Len!' she called up the stairs. 'It's gone eight o'clock.'

I watched her lift the lamb into a straw-lined orange box on the hearth and I frowned. My job after school, and twice a day at weekends, was to bottle feed the orphaned and abandoned lambs. If it survived this one was a dead cert for the crèche. I had mixed feelings. I hated the idea of a creature dying, and loved my lamb-feeding duties, but there were three animals under my care already and I only had two hands. Mother clipped my head lightly as she passed. 'Stop day dreaming young lady. You've got school.'

Len stomped down the stairs three steps at a time and through the kitchen, shrugging into his coat and hoisting his school bag onto his back without pause. I eyed that leather satchel enviously. I would have done almost anything for one of my own. Dark brown and shiny, like newly-hatched chestnuts, or would have been if it were mine. Being Len's it was scuffed and ragged from three years of secondary school playgrounds and school buses. Our father had re-stitched it many times, pulling the thick, curved needle that he kept for mending halters through the worn leather with a pair of pliers. It was a sorry excuse for a bag but still an object that I coveted.

Len threw out a mumbled, 'See you Mum,' and dived outside, dragging his bike from the woodshed and pedalling down the track for the mile long ride to the school bus-stop before he could be called back.

Mother tried though. 'Wait for Susan,' she shouted after him. 'Len!'

'He's gone,' Stan said. 'You'm wastin' your breath.'

She tutted irritably and turned back to me. 'Have you got your clean vest?'

'Oh Mum…'

'You've got PE today.'

'Yes, Mum.'

'Then have you…'

'Yes, Mum.' I looked at Dad, who rolled his eyes, and I smothered another grin. Mother's daily check list was legendary, and she did not laugh at things like clean vests; but we did – me and my Dad.

'Ash,' he said.

I nodded and smiled. The reminder wasn't needed but I was glad he thought to give it. 'I'll stop by the shaw. Plenty of stands there.'

'Hurry up then, pet. Old Dixie'll have kittens if yer late.'

I grabbed my gabardine mac, slightly damp as it always was through the winter months and into the spring, and hurried out to disinter my own bike from the shed. I only needed to cycle as far as the farmyard and on fine bright mornings that could even be a pleasure, despite negotiating potholes that could swallow half the depth of the front wheel if miss-judged.

At the bottom of the lane I slowed by the small copse that separated our lane from the main farm road. I dropped my bike on the verge and surveyed the woodland's edge. Fortunately for me this section of frith had yet to be cleared and there were plenty of saplings to be raided. I jumped across the ditch and grabbed onto a young ash standing proud from the mass of newly emerging green. It took only a moment or two to select a couple of growing tips; slender and smooth and grey, their foliage still encased in cool black buds that looked for all the world like the hooves of tiny goats.

I tucked both sprigs into my bag and knotted the string carefully. Losing them was not an option. It was Ash Wednesday, when every Sussex school child would arrive at the gates armed with the Ash. These short lengths of twig were transient in extreme but essential for surviving the day. Those lacking the Ash could expect pinched arms and stamped-on feet by all who noticed their error. And with playgrounds being what they were that could be every student on the premises before the first bell rang. Like an injured wildebeest they would become prey to the wolf pack and it had been known for the ashless to scaddle off, rather than suffer their fate. A few short hours after this the Ash would become unlucky sticks that needed to be discarded as close to midday as lessons allowed. To be caught with Ash by the dinner break would result in a fresh orgy of violence. Being opposed to pain, on the whole, I went to great lengths to prove my solidarity with tradition.

My pit stop had made me late and I needed to pedal double quick or risk a wrath of a different kind. Dixie Hope, the farm's one remaining groom, was not a morning person, despite a life time of rising at dawn to tend his beloved horses. He took myself and his daughter Babs to school every morning in the farm's Land Rover and had left without me on several occasions; arguing that he had to fetch the Guv'nor's newspapers, and he 'wouldn't wait for folks as couldn't get their arse out of bed of a morn'n.' He was perfectly correct, because without the need for fetching the Guv'nor's morning papers we would not be getting the lift at all, but Dixie's time keeping still felt a little draconian.

I hurtled into the yard just as he was backing the Land Rover out of the garage.

'You're late,' Babs called from the drive. 'We were going without you.'

Babs was very much out of place in a farmyard, being all crimped curls every day with fresh ribbons, shiny patent leather shoes and lace-edged socks. I went out of my way to be a *William* to her *Violet Elizabeth* 'So?' I said. 'Wouldn't have to go to school then would I?'

She only tossed her head. 'You'd get the cane, you would. So there.'

I limited myself to a surreptitious shove as Babs stepped delicately up into the cab. She turned and sneered at me. 'You'm got muddy boots. Dad says you've gotta go in the back.' She tugged the door closed and smirked through the window. As I preferred not to sit next to her I was happy to climb into the back and we headed out across Sawyers Common to Haltwood Primary School.

We arrived with half an hour to go before the bell. With Ash Day tyranny in the offing the playground was unusually busy for that hour. Babs rushed off to see her cronies whilst I made for the cloakroom to change my wellington-boots for school browns. The cloakroom smelled as it always did, of old socks and wet coats, with a faint undertone of farmyard, but it was warm. I lingered for a few minutes, taking extra care over my shoelaces before retrieving my precious ash twigs.

The larger of the sticks was tucked into the top of my right sock, making sure it was both well secured and prominently displayed. The other I rammed into my pocket as an emergency backup. Thievery was not unknown, either by stealth or overt mugging. The wise and windy would always carry a spare.

I reached the steps leading down to the playground and used their vantage point to gauge the mood. Voices were raised in chanting, accompanied by the rhythmic slap of rope against tarmac, telling me that Angie Cartwright's skipping corner was already active. I considered joining in except for the fact that Angie was a villager and though we bore no personal grudges each of us knew that Villagers and Commoners did not mix. It was an ancient rule; never voiced but always obeyed. Nobody quite knew why.

I was half way down the steps to playground level when Bobby Fuller issued me the challenge.

'Ash,' he called. 'Ash or bash!'

I turned my leg awkwardly to display the twig. 'Got mine,' I said loudly. 'Have you?'

'Course,' He replied. 'Peter Marshall hasn't though. Adam Garton dead legged 'im.' He grinned at me. 'Got yer marbles?'

I shook my head. Marbles season always saw the boys in a frenzy. Marbles were a serious business but I hadn't the stomach for their fierce tournaments that would carry on until Easter and which were the basis for many a grazed knee, bruised arm or worse. Bobby shrugged and moved off to join the kneeling gaggle of players.

I looked around for a sign of the unfortunate Peter. I would add my time-honoured blow to Ash if a victim was under my nose but I didn't seek them out. Bobby was a real bully, as was Adam. I was glad that both kept contact with me down to taunts about my size. They left me alone because Len was a Scout patrol leader; and Len was a lot bigger than either of them. It was small change as bullying went. I ignored them and they ignored me and all was good.

''Lo Sue.'

I turned to see my best friend, Linda, crouching on the steps. 'H'lo Lin. You got yours then?' I said, striding up to her and pointing at my ash twig.

Linda glanced about her nervously. 'Fer'got,' she whispered.

I drew an exaggerated breath, slapped my left hand over my mouth in mock horror, and reached my right hand into my pocket to tweak the spare ash tip into her palm. It was the same smooth grey, starkly marked with far fewer matt-black buds and far smaller than the piece I had kept myself, but was Ash, nevertheless.

She curled her fingers over it like a slow gin trap. 'Ooh, thanks, Sue.' She bent quickly and slid the twig into her sock before flinging both arms around me. 'I was thinkin' I were a deader there, then.'

''Salright,' I said 'Here, you never guess what. Last night...' I stopped. Dad had made me promise, but the poachers were so tempting to tell on. 'We got a lamb in our oven,' I ended. 'A real live one.'

'Were it orfinned?' Linda asked.

'Dunno.' I shrugged, feeling a little stupid. Rejected lambs were commonplace, and not something to get exited over. I felt slightly embarrassed. 'Got yer rope?' I asked finally.

'Yer ... tis.' Linda shook out her tangle of clothes line, tied one end to the fence and played the rest out across the tarmac. 'You first,' she said, a sure sign of her gratitude when the rope-owner always had first dibs. She began to turn the rope, slowly at first with exaggerated windmilling of her right arm. The cord billowed into a flowing arc, and slapped the ground, lightly at first, steadily building to the air-cracking rhythm required for serious play.

Another *Commoner* wandered across to loiter expectantly next to Linda. 'Can I join?' she asked.

'If'n you turns first, Mags.' Linda handed over the cord-end without further comment and went to stand opposite me. As if by arrangement three more girls drifted up. One untied the tethered end and the rope suddenly turned easier for being guided by human hands. The lines of waiting girls swelled to four a side, all watching the rope, each gauging the speed with a practised eye, each one a paid-up expert on the unwritten physics of the skipping-rope.

I bent down to push my ash twig further into my sock, and smiled as Linda mirrored my movement.

'Teddy bear on three,' I shouted, 'One... Two... THREE!'

We leapt into the rope's blurred ellipse and began to skip and mime, whilst the assembled girls chanted.

Teddy bear, teddy bear, turn around,
Teddy bear, teddy bear, touch the ground,
Teddy bear, teddy bear, brush your hair,
Teddy bear, teddy bear, climb the stair,
Teddy bear, teddy bear, reach for the sky,
Teddy bear, teddy bear, wave goodbye,
Teddy bear, teddy bear, turn off the light,
Teddy bear, teddy bear, say goodnight.

*

We only had a lift into school and had to find our own way home, and as there were no buses across the common at that hour this inevitably fell to Shanks's Pony. My mother would arrive at the school gates by 3.30pm on her ancient Raleigh bicycle. Quite a number of local mothers told their offspring to walk with her; some of them without asking, much to my mother's annoyance. It was not uncommon for a crocodile of a dozen or more kids to set off with us from the school gates in a noisy clump. The expedition steadily decreased in numbers until only she and I were left for the last half mile to the end of our lane and we seldom arrived home much under an hour after leaving the school gates.

Now I had past the infant class stage, and on the days when there were extra guests at the big house to clean for, Mother would not always be able to reach the gates by school-closing. On those occasions I would let the rest of the pack tear off across the common ahead of me and dawdle the three miles to the main farm absorbed in my new library book. There I would collect my bike and ride the last half mile to our house.

To get from yard and house I first needed to negotiate the shaw at the mouth of the cart track. These trees formed a dark archway for several hundred yards and for some reason it always seemed darker from the 'road end'; perhaps because the *sheer-way* sloped upwards from there, or maybe after a day of school my tired mind was more open to suggestion. Whatever the reason I invariably paused to peer along the path, listening to the small snaps and rustles in the frith and imagining all of the Knuckers and Farisees that might be lurking there, waiting to pounce.

Home and tea could only be reached through that leafy tunnel, however, and at the time of year, when the sun was already dipping past the trees, I wasn't keen to hang around. The only option was to take a deep breath, stand on the bicycle's pedals, and make a dash for it.

Once beyond it I slowed down. The flint track rose sharply and kept rising for most of the way home. My ancient bike was heavy, and even the Sturmer Archer three-speed hub didn't make the pedalling so very much easier. Often I would end up pushing it the last hundred yards, but I was on home ground now, and safe. The lane was as familiar as my own garden, if a little wilder. Grass in March was still brown and lank in places, not yet springing with any speed, but that did leave room for swathes of primroses and milkmaids and a scattering of violets and celandines along the ditches and banks.

Once I reached flatter ground, with the sun rapidly disappearing and too cold to linger, I pedalled the last stretch with head down, often against a prevailing south-easterly wind that shuddered through and around the hedges and trees on either side. By the time our cottage was in sight, with its whitewashed walls and black framed windows gleaming in the early spring sunlight, I would be breathing hard, and ready for tea.

I scraped my boots off my feet outside the lean-to porch

and stomped into the kitchen, glancing toward the Aga. Its door was closed, with the black enamelled kettle rocking gently on a well heated hob. 'Where's the lamb gone, Mum?'

'Gone up to middle-close. Your Dad's got a heat lamp set up for it,' Mum replied. 'I can't be having sheep in the house. You're late,' she added. 'And your Dad needs some tea taking up to him but our Len's not in yet.'

'I'll go,' I said.

'Are you sure? It's getting dark.'

'I knows the way.'

My mother pursed her lips. She didn't like me going back out in the dusk chill but knew she had little option. 'Go and change, then. And be quick.'

I never needed very much excuse to help my father with the stock, especially at lambing time. Within ten minutes I was trotting up the lane toward the middle close with a basket containing flasks of soup and tea, a packet of bread and butter and a thick chunk of fruitcake. The track on that side of our cottage was not bike friendly. Being so little used it was not maintained. It was probably an indication of how most roads would have been before metalled roads had become the norm. Once it had led across to the Haven and been a well-used route from the Billingshurst road to the locks that connected canal to river. But with the canal's demise and the building of the flood control weir on the Arun it was an effective dead end for half a century or more and had been demoted from road to bridle path or sheer-way

It was a short walk, downhill and another rise up to the barns, along a muddy, potholed, sheer-way. But delicate health had left me small for my age and I had to pause several times to rest my basket on the verge to catch my breath, but those pauses were never wasted time. The lane was well into the long shadows of dusk by then and the sounds of evening were in full flow. Sheep and lambs called to each other as they settled for the night. A blackbird vied with a neighbouring robin for volume, to pipe the sun's exit. I strained my neck to catch sight of the songsters. The blackbird was perched high in an ash tree that was still bare of leaves; the robin I could not trace, though he was closest to me. I picked up the basket and moved on.

At the top of the hill the track ran through a collection of farm buildings generally known as the middle close. On one side a Sussex barn, on the other stood its gangly Dutch cousin. Beyond that point the flint lane became little more than a muddy, grassed space between hedges, plied by no vehicles other than the occasional tractor as it wound on to the distant Top Close.

A Sussex barn dominated a selection of low sheds and outhouses constructed from stone, brick and tarred planking. The group formed three sides of a yard, which was completed by a brick wall and gate. Beyond the Dutch barn lay another sloping woodland, larger than the shaw at the main-road end, which protected the whole confab from wet south-westerlies.

Sheep and lambs corralled within the yard were singing the same pathetic calls as their field-companions. Now that lambing was almost finished my father had the last remaining un-lambed ewes in the lower sheds where there was power and water and shelter for the new-borns. These stragglers in the lambing season were mostly young shearlings, or old matriarch cullers.

In contrast with the evening air, which was rapidly chilling out in the lane, it was warm inside. The sheds were dimly lit by a single bulb above the pens. The smell of straw and the sharp tangy odour of sheep made me sneeze.

My father was sitting on some bales watching an old ewe laying in the straw at his feet. She was barely moving but for her heaving chest. I could see she was in distress and also see the concern in my father's expression. But when he turned at the sound of the door clicking shut behind me he smiled.

''Lo Dad,' I called, softly because he had always taught us not to shout around animals, and new mothers in particular.

He beckoned, nodding approval. 'Put the bait in the store,'

he said quietly.

I trotted through to the small room where he kept bins of feed, tools and veterinary supplies, and set the basket down on a stool. Our collie-dog, Bo, waited there, curled on a hessian sack, knowing he was not welcome in the lambing pens. He raised his head sleepily as my fingers ploughed through his fox-brown ruff and he flapped his tail a few times.

I noted the light in the corner and went to peer at the tiny lamb nestled in its small pen. A heat lamp was poised above him as he slept. I reached out to touch his oily, wiry, coat, so different to how most people imagine a lamb to be. The little animal did not wake.

Bo watched my every move, a quiet, rumbling rising deep within him. He was placed on guard by the master, and though as a family member he would never harm me he was still a working dog and never a pet. I knew not to take any liberties, or confuse him with conflicting demands.

''Salright boy, I won't hurt it.' I rubbed Bo's head fleetingly and hurried back to the main shed. Dad was crouched by the ewe, his hands buried in the thick, greasy wool covering her flanks.

'Is she bad,' I asked.

He nodded. 'I'm afraid so, pet. She's an old yowe, and she was holdin' three lambs this time.' He pointed at the two small bodies already huddled in the straw.

I edged around, careful not to worry the mother with sudden movements, and bent to stroke the new-borns. One of them opened its mouth, emitting a tiny bleat. It struggled to rise on shaky legs and staggered toward me, butting into my knees with surprising power for an animal not yet an hour old. I let it suck at my fingers. 'He's hungry,' I said. 'Shall I mix some bottles?'

'Can you manage enough of them? I can't leave the old girl here just now.'

'Course I can do it. Little blue scoop in the milk powder tub. Four level scoops to every pint.'

Dad laughed. 'Off you go then, duck. There's the biddy one in the store under the lamp. He's already had a feed so don't let him tell you otherwise. And you be careful with that kettle.'

'Oh Dad. I'm not a bab...' I began. He was not listening. His entire attention was fixed on his sickly charge. I gave the ewe a long look. She was still panting rapidly, woolly sides heaving in and out with the effort. Her tongue lolled from her black muzzle and her yellow, slitted eyes were unfocussed and staring. I turned away, willing the mother to live for her new children, but knowing that in such a poor state survival was unlikely. 'I'll get the bottles,' I muttered, and crept away.

In the store, I kept my mind from the inevitable with the mixing of milk powder. Frothy, pale liquid sent cloying steam into my face and I wrinkled my nose as it always smelled vaguely musty, not like milk at all.

A row of glistening clean beer bottles stood on the bench with cotton wool tucked into their tops to keep out the dust. Filling the bottles was easy but I always had trouble with the rubber teats. Being a deliberate tight fit to stop greedy lambs swallowing them, the rubber would begin to stretch, and then snap back across my fingers. I had dropped bottles before now because of that. Just for once the rubber slid down the neck easily and I laughed in triumph. I fixed the other and stood both bottles in a bucket of cold water to cool them.

An odd noise from the barn distracted me. I looked at Bo and frowned. The dog had heard the same sounds and was standing with his nose pressed against the crack of the door. His feathery tail was tucked between his haunches and he whined quietly, with ears laid back and his dense coat trembling. His anxiety reached out to me, making my hair itch.

'Bo?'

The dog glanced over his shoulder, tongue flickering nervously around his muzzle. Beyond the door sheep were making their usual sheep noises. Straw was rustling beneath cloven feet. I could hear the low murmur of a voice; my father talking to his charges, as he always did. Yet something had to be wrong for the stoic Bo to get in such a lather.

I went to the door, catching Bo's collar as I opened it wider. My father was kneeling by the ewe, but not talking to her. He was directing his comments to her lambs in a quiet monologue that I could not quite make out. My father pulled the ewe onto her back. Her head flopped to one side, her tongue lolling in a flaccid lump.

I backed into the store and pushed Bo onto the hessian. 'Sit,' I whispered at him. 'Stay.'

The dog rolled his eyes but obeyed, still grumbling under his breath.

Grabbing the bucket containing the bottles I crept back through the door, closing it quietly behind me.

My father looked grim, almost angry, which frightened me more than anything else could when he never raised his voice to me – ever. I hunched between some straw bales and watched as he took out his penknife. Honed to a wafer thin edge, the large knife was his all-purpose toolkit. Hoof-trimmer, twine-cutter and a dozen other things besides and always in his pocket ready for use. He looked down at the ewe for several seconds. The ewe was quite obviously dead, so what could he possibly do now?

I held my breath and rose up onto my knees for a better view. I watched my father's knife slice along the ewe's swollen belly and I drew breath, expecting blood and guts to pour out onto the straw. Instead, I saw a silvery sack, streaked with blood, yes, but not pouring gore. Not yet. It was the next cut which did that as he pierced the membrane and dragged a tiny lamb from its mother's belly.

My own stomach felt as though it were flip-flopping with an acute and sudden nausea. I could hardly believe my father would do such a thing, yet I could not look away.

My father was ripping a slimy layer from the lamb and rubbing its chest. 'Bugger,' he muttered. 'Breathe. Come on.'

The slippery body lay as motionless as its mother. He picked it up and blew into its mouth a few times, still rubbing its chest. Then he rose, lifted the lamb by its back legs, and swung it back and fore. 'Cough it up you liddle bugger,' he shouted. 'Come on bwoy. Spit it out.'

From where I crouched in the straw he seemed to have gone totally mad.

Then he was on his knees once again, rubbing the lamb vigorously with handfuls of straw, and talking to it in soft, soothing tones. It struggled feebly, wobbling to its feet. It opened its tiny black muzzle – and protested its violent awakening.

Still I crouched in the bales, staring between the bloody carcass, the three lambs, and my father. 'Is she dead?' I whispered at last, knowing the answer but having to ask, just to be sure.

My father twisted around to look at me, smiling a little sadly. 'The yowe? Yes.' He bowed his head for a few moments, and then looked me full in the face. I could see his eyes were moist, and felt the tension dissipating, knowing that my father was as sad as I was.

'Come here, Pet,' he said quietly.

I dragged the bucket with the bottles into the small arena of light; hesitating as my gaze fixed on his blood stained hands.

'Tis what 'appens,' he said, gesturing at the dead sheep. He took the bucket from me and stood the bottles on the ground before plunging his hands into the water. 'I had to get the lamb out or it would die an' all.'

I nodded, still not speaking, feeling numbed and confused. The lambs would live, and I'd seen dead sheep many times. Just not this way.

My father washed the gore from his hands and dried them on some straw before he pulled me to him. I snuggled deep into his arms, squeezing my eyes tight shut. 'Not nice is it?' he said, gently. 'But it happens. She was a very old lady, in sheep years, and she wasn't up to triplets.' He pushed me away far enough to grab one of the bottles and tip a little milk onto his wrist. 'That's cooled down nicely. You want to feed en?'

I nodded, not trusting myself to speak for fear of releasing the tidal wave pushing at the back of my eyeballs.

He counted the bottles. 'Only two? I tell you what. We'll share this around. They won't drink a pint each tonight. That sound okay?'

I nodded again, managing a pale smile and followed him into the store. Bo was waiting with his nose pressed against the door. He was crowding my father's legs, whining gently. My father ruffled his ears and signalled him back to his sacking bed with a rapid hand movement. 'I'll be back in a minute,' my father said.

I took down a third bottle a small funnel to share the milk round, and as I worked I could hear the noises from next door of something being moved across the straw and heard the far doors of the barn open and shut a few seconds later. I knew he was disposing of the carcass.

When he returned he poured hot water into a bucket and, grabbing an eroded bar of carbolic soap, scrubbed at his hands for a second time. 'Ready?' he asked. He grabbed the bottles and led me back into the barn.

I paused just for a moment in the doorway, looking toward the place where the ewe had been. There was only fresh litter. Curled up on the spot, were three very much alive lambs.

Tucking one of them under my arm I offered it the bottle. The lamb mumbled the teat around for a moment or two before biting toothless gums onto the soft rubber. It sucked, skinny tail beginning to wiggle as the warm milk trickled down its throat. I fell into familiar routine as a panacea.

'His name's Sam,' I said. 'Can I keep him?'

My father hesitated. 'Well, he's not mine to give, Poppet, but you can help feed him. I'll have to bring en up to the house anyway, four of en with the one from this morning, so you can feed them when you get in from school. Alright?'

'Okay.' I hugged the lamb to me, and it lost its grip on the teat. It bleated, loudly, until I jammed its mouth full once more.

Birch Sap and Raisin Wine

1 gall of birch sap

3 lemons

4 lb of raisins

2 ½ lb of loaf sugar

1 oz of almonds

Method

1. Stone the raisins and place them in a crock.
2. Blanch and chop the almonds, peel the lemons thinly.
3. Place them all in a pan with the sugar.
4. Add the birch sap (with extra water to make a gallon if needed).
5. Heat the pan's contents until it boils and then simmer for 20 minutes.
6. Strain the liquid and pour it over the raisins.
7. Cover the crock and leave for 14 days or until fermentation has quietened. Strain and pour into a demijohn with an air-lock.
8. When fermentation has finished bottle the wine and store in a rack for at least one year.

Medicinal

I must say that I have no idea whether you can claim that fermented products have the same medicinal values as the raw materials, but if you think they help – all the better.

Birch sap wine was supposedly made popular by the Prince Regent. It was certainly renowned in some areas, including Sussex, as a potent tonic.

As an herbal remedy natural birch is a bitter compound that stimulates appetite. It is also an astringent and an anti-rheumatic.

Birch sap is also said to be good for the skin.

You can use the sap in early spring to sweeten drinks.

It has been said that birch-leaf infusions will break up kidney stones.

Traditional

In folklore birch was well known as a deterrent against witches and other evils or ill lucks. It was common, at one time, to find garlands made from birch, may, rowan and cowslips in kitchens, barns and even worn around hats, to ward off evil.

It was used often in churches on Whit Sunday and was chosen (it is said) because the new growth represented new life, and the rustling sound made by the fine shoots and branches in often drafty churches symbolised the sound of the Holy Spirit rushing down on the Apostles.

Birch was also a fertility symbol. With the tradition of 'jumping' a broomstick made of birch set across the doorway of a newly-wed's home, it both symbolised marriage and conception of a first-born.

In pagan traditions it is held to be the tree of new beginnings and protection of the young and also as a Wiccan tree of lunar magic.

Birch brooms would never be made at Yuletide or during the Goddess's month of May.

It is also said that no record exists of anyone being struck by lightening when sheltering under a birch tree.

Cowslips & the Gorgon

I hated travelling by car at the best of times, so the scant twenty five miles from the Sussex Weald into the South Downs crammed into a Mini-van without seats and no way of getting fresh air was a torture. I am willing to bet it was almost as much agony for the rest of the family. I demanded to know if we were *nearly there yet* at two minute intervals from the moment we left the farm drive until we pulled into Saddlescombe Farm, close to the Devil's Dyke. Yet I was willing to suffer the discomfort of any trip to see Auntie Joan. Joan was my father's sister, and my favourite aunt. Going there was always an entertainment.

Like many of our friends and neighbours we had no vehicle of our own. The van belonged to the Colonel, who occupied the only other house in our lane. My father and brother mowed lawns and other odd jobs in return for the occasional loan of his Austin Mini-Van.

When we finally arrived Len and I piled out as rapidly as we were able to stretch cramped limbs in the warm sun. Saddlescombe was so much more open than the heavily wooded farmland were we lived. The Downlands opened up to greater expanses of sky. A near constant wind came from Brighton, up and over the Devil's Dyke and even on the calmest day there was always enough to ruffle my hair.

I gazed around at gently insistent chalk slopes of the coombe that were like speckled velvet, cropped smooth by rabbits and sheep. Here and there was a stand of gorse and bramble and wild clematis, with an occasional white chalk scar marking a rabbit warren or path. It was something I could look at any old day. This trip was not about scenery, however. It was all about Aunt Joan.

I ran down the track, passing the splash-pond and casting a wary glance at the gander cruising across the water toward me, and stopped at a garden door set in the high flint wall surrounding our aunt's garden. I thumbed the latch of the flaking green gate and stepped into one of my favourite places in the universe.

My aunt's garden spoke to me from the pages of a dozen books that I had read and cherished; specifically it was just how I imagined F Hodgson Burnett's *Secret Garden* would look. The wall to my left was built from the same flint and brick as that which I had just passed through. To my right a line of sheds were set into the slope, with a short wall on the roof to prevent anyone from the lane beyond it from straying in. The fourth side of the hidden garden was the cottage itself. A straight path led from gate to door, with a chaos of shaggy lawn and straggling shrubs to the left, whilst a military spread of fine tilth marched off to the right; the kitchen garden dug and prepared for the coming season. Closest to the gate were neat rows of fruit bushes filling the sunny south end with the vaguely acrid scent of blackcurrants. The walls themselves to south and west were covered with what would have been espaliered apple, plum and pear trees had aunt and uncle been that precise. What there were was a maze of wires and branches, flushed here and there with pink-tinged blossom.

'Hellooooo my dears.' Aunt Joan's husky voice preceded her through the door as she hustled out to greet us, her wispy, greying bun whipped free by wind of its pins and grips which valiantly fought to keep the candyfloss mass under control.

She stood, with arms wide, waiting to meet my headlong rush. I hugged myself against her, realising that in my eleventh year I was already as tall as she. Her flour-strewn wrap-over pinny smelled of jam and vanilla essence and I knew without asking that Aunt Joan was baking. It was a semi-permanent state for her during the summer months. Friends and family used her cottage as a welcoming tea-shop on their way back from a trip to the nearby town of Brighton. Enticing wafts of cakes and cheese scones drifted from the kitchen, promising much of the ritual that was in those days a farmhouse Sunday tea.

'Come in my dears,' she wheezed. 'Kettle's just on. I've got some biscuits made. Oooh lovely, thank you, Stan.' She took the bunch of late daffodils that my father had plucked from his garden. 'I'll fetch some water for en d'rectly... Now, Len, there's biscuits in the barrel on the dresser. Mickey's upstairs. Go up an' see him if you like. Tell him we're all going out now, so he c'n come down and put his wellies on.'

With no space left for replies in her breathless monologue Len could only nod and flee in search of our cousin, Michael. I reached under the table and scooped up Joan's one-eyed cat who, rather obviously, and somewhat macabrely, rejoiced in the name of Blinky. I soothed his long, slightly matted, chocolate-brown fur, and waited. Aunt Joan always had something planned and I was not disappointed.

'I've got a little job needs doing,' Joan began. 'Dave'll be a while today. They're moving Gorgon, and he c'n be an 'andful. Should've done it yesterday, but they had a whole coach load of hikers traipsin' through – roight when they didn't need en – an' you know what that old Gorgon's like about visitors.'

I let Blinky slide from my hands to the floor. This sounded more than promising. Gorgon was a bull with a pedigree longer than the page it was written on. He sired prize-winning calves and earned his keep ten times over, but he was commonly agreed to be a bad'n'. Foul tempered, tetchy and unpredictable, he wore a lead mask when out in public that prevented him seeing anything beyond his feet; the theory being that he would not charge what he could not see.

I knew differently. Plenty of things annoyed him. No one thing in particular, just things. People talking; people not talking; people walking or not walking; bushes rustling; birds hopping. Just things in general. I also knew from personal observation that when Gorgon was annoyed by these small irritations in his life he would, regardless of obscured vision, lower his head and charge.

I had heard my father telling others on our home farm how three men had felt the wrong end of Gorgon's vile temper on different occasions, and how each had ended up in the casualty ward. According to my father one more attack, on anyone, and he'd be 'leaving Easy Street for the knacker's yard'. I had no idea where Easy Street was, though I could hazard a fair guess. I knew all too much about the knacker's yard. It was where the old and sick animals went to die. It was rumoured at school that these were then destined to become the contents of the corned beef tart we were often fed with in the school dining hall.

Joan had slipped out of her apron and grabbed her cardigan from the back of a kitchen chair. 'Oven's off. I c'n clear up later,' she said. 'The paigles are full out. An' what with the bit o' sun we've had, I thought we'd go up on the Dyke an' pick some. If that's all roight by you people?'

'Fine.' My father grinned. 'Just the paigles, Joan?'

'Not much else about now, Stan. Though I did reck'n I'd stretch to some elder flowers a bit later on.' She scooped up two wicker baskets and handed one to me. 'Here,' she said. 'You take one an' I'll 'ave t'other. All right, my duck?'

I nodded, and slipped out of the door behind her. I loved going up to the Devil's Dyke. It was no different to the rest of the South Downs really, but the tales of devil's pacts and demonic curses had a wonderful thrill to them. It was a place where imagination ran riot because of the very name; and where the reality, with its conical centre and deep surrounding ditch, was almost as good.

Everybody had started up the pathway and though I was impatient that they would not get too far ahead I was also eager to enjoy my favourite aunt's company without the others to distract her. I held back to walk beside her. 'Tell me the stories Auntie Joan,' I pleaded as she carefully locked the door. 'Tell me about the Devil's digging.'

'Again?' Joan laughed and slipped her hand under my elbow to link arms as we walked up toward the chalk-track.

'Aren't you gettin' a bit old fer all that m'dear?'

I grinned and shook my head. I loved to hear the old tales of the surrounding Sussex hills and never tired of them though I'd heard them all a dozen times over since I was old enough to take them in.

'All right then, ducky. That'd be the tale of old Saint Cuthman I'm guessing. Of course he weres'n't a saint back then. He were just a shepherd. Loike your old dad. Kept his sheep up on the Downs just the same. And he looked after his ol' mother. He did build the church at Steyning, they do tell.' She paused to motion me over the stile. 'Take the baskets, Susie,' she said. Once on the other side we began to climb steadily upwards. 'Now then, where was I?'

'Saint Cuthman,' I said. 'How he built the church.'

'And so he did, ducky. He'd be doing miracles as well if they'm made him a saint, but I can't say as I know what they were.' Joan glanced at me and grinned. 'Still, it wurse a long while back now an' I bain't that old. Anyway. Old Cuthman helped build a nunnery on the hills, right where the Dyke is. One day, when he was just finishing off, Old Nick turns up an' he says, 'Cuthman, you'm wasting your time there lad. I'm letting the sea up this biddy bit tonight. Well, old Cuthman wasn't having any of that, so he goes and talks to Mother Superior, an' he tells 'er what Old Nick's been sayin'. 'You get your nuns a prayin',' he tells her, 'an' when it's midnight you'm light up the church with everything you'm got.' So they does, and when Old Nick turns up that evenin' and starts diggin' he hears them prayin' but he takes no notice, cos he's a daft old Robbutt really.'

She looked at me, squinting against the sun, and I realised for the second time that day that I really was taller than she; which was not hard when she, like her mother and her own aunts, was barely five feet tall in her socks. The thought distracted me for a moment. I had the terrible notion that if Joan noticed my height she would stop telling this 'adult' niece her wonderful tales.

'Well, then. What 'appens next d'you suppose?' Joan was asking me.

I shook my head, though I knew the story perfectly well.

'Wahl. It gets to midnight, and them they nuns lights up the church. And the chickens thinks its daytime comin', so the rooster, he starts up with his noise. Old Nick, now, he knows he has to be back under the hill before the sun, so when he hears them roosters he throws down his shovel and he runs for cover. He never did finish the Dyke, but we've still got the bit he'd dug.' She paused for us to climb the next stile.

'He does come back though,' I urged her, grabbing the baskets once more as Joan climbed after me.

'Does he now?' Joan stared at me for a moment before taking the baskets and setting off up the final slopes to the top of the Dyke. 'Now maybe so m'duck. He only sets a hoof up here when folks does it roight. You 'ave to run round the dyke seven times, widdershins, on Midsummer's Eve, and then you'll meet him coming t'other way...'

'With his porridge,' I laughed.

'That's roight. Gurt big bowl of it.'

'An' you musn't eat it,' I shrieked.

'So they tells us,' Joan agreed.

'If you don't eat it he can't touch you,' I said, giggling now.

'As roight. In fact, if you don't eat it, he has to do whatever you says until the sun comes up again. I reck'n you knows this story as well as I do.' She stopped at the head of the rise and looked down into the deep culvert that formed the Devil's Dyke. 'Here we are,' she said. 'Roight on the edge.'

I stood beside her and gazed at the huge cleft in the hillside, and at the expanse of the South Downs that rolled for miles under a clear, sun-bathed sky. In the distance a faint glitter hinted of the English Channel. The slopes that lay between were dotted with gorse and bramble patches clothed in sprawling cloaks of old man's beard. Between the chalky screes sheep and cattle were keeping vigil in their own sections of springy turf, with heads down, steadily mowing the grass into a short and spongy green carpet sprinkled with a haze of spring flowers. Most common, after daisies, were the delicate, nodding bells of butter-yellow cowslips that Sussex-folk called paigles.

I looked along the cleft of the dyke to where it curved out of sight; steep, mysterious, full of dark shadows at its base. Even on this bright day I could imagine all manner of things lurking there. 'One day,' I said, 'I'm going to do that. Run round it at midnight an' see if that old devil does come out the top.'

'Will you, then?' Joan laughed. 'I wouldn't if I was you. He's not nice. Got bad breath an' all. And anyway, there's some hereabouts that do say that little tale might be proper for the tree ring over Chanctonbury way. So you'd be wasting a lot o' puff my gal.'

'Oh.' I regarded her for a moment. I was fooling around but from her tone I could not help wondering if she were being serious. She seemed quite so, but was that because she thought I was my younger self, and still open to seeing truth in the old tales? Or that she herself believed in a miracle-wielding saint? Not wanting to upset her either way I nodded. 'All right then. I'll leave it til I'm bigger.'

'I would,' Joan agreed, her face solemn, though her eyes glittered with laughter.

And then the moment was passed. Len came running up to thrust a bunch of cowslips at us. 'Do you want all of these, Aunt Joan?' he demanded.

'Just the blossoms, love.' Joan put one basket on the grass and took the bunch from him. 'Like this.' She stripped the deep-yellow fragrant blooms into the wicker basket.

Len stared at them, a little chagrined by how small a scattering his bunch had made across the woven base. 'How many do we have to pick?' he asked.

'A gallon,' Joan replied.

'A gallon of flowers?' He was scornful. 'You don't get

flowers in gallons. You'm gets milk in gallons.'

'Oh yes you do, my lad. I'll show you d'rectly, when we gets back.' She ruffled his hair. 'Go on with you.'

The warm afternoon passed quickly and quietly as we worked across the Dyke. The whole family picked steadily, or at least the three adults did. Len and Mickey grew bored after half an hour and wandered off to see who could throw stones clear across the Dyke at an outcrop of chalk laid bare by a landslip. I also tired of picking and stripping after an hour; even though I loved their sweet, fresh, apricot smell. I became side-tracked by another favourite pastime of my own. Daisy chains. Within a half hour I had several necklets and coronets of perky white flowers, twined here and there with yellow buttercups and sea pinks and even a few early scabious with their fluffy blue heads that I found irresistible.

Oblivious to the smiles and nods of my elders I was happy, and flitted to and fro across the Downland, trilling a rather flat rendition of some song I'd heard on *Children's Favourites*. Indoors my a-tonal warbling would have attracted cat-calls from the family, but out there, with competing with the larks and pewits, they could only smile.

'Oh, my.' Joan suddenly straightened up, peering at her watch. 'It's late. Dave'll be in from milkin' soon.' She trotted across to my father and dumped her basket at his feet. 'We don't need many more, but can you finish off while I go an' get the tea on?'

'Of course,' he said. 'Cost you though … you've got to take young Susie with you.'

'Roight oh. Come on Suzie-sunshine.'

I ran up to her and swung one of my long flower chains around her neck. 'Have we got lemon carts?' I asked.

'I'm not sure we have,' Joan replied, shooting Stan a warning look.

I smiled to myself. One of the stories my father loved to recount was that of 'the lemon curd tarts'. Joan was prone to spoonerisms and on one afternoon, after some teasing from

Stan and two of his navy cohorts, she had walked into a wartime bakers shop devoid of almost all confections, to innocently request, 'six lemon turd carts, please'. The family legend told how Joan, mortified by the gaff, had fled and refused to go back for the rest of the war years.

Joan sniffed her disgust, and quit the field of conflict, unwilling to parry words with her quick-tongued younger brother. I know she loved him dearly, but he was a joker and always got the better of her. I was also thrilled at having teased my aunt so successfully if a little chagrined to think I may have offended her.

We hurried down the hill, faster on the return journey, and climbed the stile to walk briskly through the lower meadow. Across the field I could see Uncle David's wiry outline by the gate at the next stile, with a taller man by his side.

'Well now,' Joan mused, 'I wonder what they'm wantin' for. I'm not that late with tea.'

She tutted impatiently, but quickened her pace, so that I almost ran to keep up with her. As we drew closer I recognised the man with Uncle Dave as the farm foreman. Both stood unnaturally still, and Joan slowed up, puzzled.

She raised a hand in greeting. 'Hello,' she called. 'What's up then, Dave?'

'Come 'ere and we'll tell you,' David replied, his voice oddly flat.

Joan stopped walking and placed both hands on her hips. 'Now what're you up to? Come on, I knows when you're up to somethin'.'

'Its fine Joan,' the foreman called out. 'Keep walking, but steady now, don't 'urry.'

Joan stepped forward cautiously. After her brother's teasing she suspected some other prank was under way.

'Hello Susie,' Uncle David said quietly. 'Keep up with Auntie now, and keep lookin' at me. It's a game. Starin' contest. See who gives up first... But you'm, got to keep walkin'.'

'Okay.' This was an old game that I thought I had grown out of, but for old time's sake I fixed my uncle with my best 'staring-out' face; with eyes saucer-wide, the skin on my face rigidly taut.

We reached the edge of the field and David unhitched the gate very slowly. He did not open it until we had got right up to him, and even then pushed it open a scant eighteen inches. We had barely slid through before he was slamming it shut behind us.

David fished for his baccy tin and lifted out a half-smoked roll-up, which he lit with evident pleasure.

It was then that I noticed a movement behind the metal bars of the gate. A gentle puffing noise told me that the *movement* was a large animal. I peered through the bars and drew a sharp breath. I was not so young to be beyond realising the potential in what had occurred.

On the far side of the gate, snorting against the lead shield that covered his face, Gorgon the bull was scenting for the intruders that had dared to cross his territory. Denied sight he had used his broad, wet nose and well furred ears to follow us across the field.

Joan stared at the animal for a moment. 'Oh. Whal then,' she said finally, and then began to laugh. Silently at first, her shoulders heaving up and down, eyes tightly closed. Then her breath, forced from her lungs in machine gun spurts, giving vent to a long string of husky hee-hee-hee's. I looked at her for a moment, and then I too began to smile. I couldn't help it. When Joan laughed, the world joined in.

David smiled, but in a wry fashion. He had been seriously frightened for us, and was not up to laughing with her just yet.

'Oh dear,' Joan said finally, wiping her eyes with the back of her hand. 'Stan and Marg are comin' down directly. They won't know ol' Gorgon's out.'

'I'll go up. Bring en down the whapple,' David said, taciturn, as always.

'Will you be all right Joan?' the foreman asked.

'Yes thanks, Bert,' Joan replied. 'Though I can't say it didn't shake me a mite. Old Gorgon trippin' across the field behind me. Can't think why I didn't hear 'im.'

They watched me trying to feed strands of flower chains to the bull without actually putting my fingers through the bars, and all the while keeping up a constant stream of chatter to calm the animal, as my father had taught me.

''Ere you are, you old devil. D'you loike grass? I betcha do. ''Ave another bit. Look, this'n's got seeds on already. Is that good then?'

The two metal rings in his nose clanked against the gate as he stretched his neck out to gain my scent. He shook his head, his mask crashing along the bars. I jumped back, scolding the beast roundly for startling me. With the gate between me and the bull I felt safe enough, but his breath was coming in louder puffs and I could tell he was revving up for a paddy.

'I can tell she's related to you Joan. Talk the donkey out and back agin' that one,' Bert said.

'She's a poppet,' Joan replied, defensive, though she knew Bert was joking. 'She's our Stan's youngest.'

'Really? She don't look like him much.'

'No,' Joan agreed. 'Marg says 'ow she's took after her young sister, Dorothy. I wouldn't know, I'm sure. Poor Dot got took with diphtheria back in thirty-four.'

Bert tipped his cap, edging away very slowly. He didn't have time to let Joan get started on one of her long tales when he had work to do still. 'Most likely,' he said. 'Now if you're fine, I'll be off. Evenin' to you, Joan.'

'See you then, Bert.'

Gorgon bellowed at the raised voices and I shrank back, giving the gate a wide berth as I joined my aunt. He was a stupid old bull anyway; didn't want to eat any of my flowers.

We walked toward the cottage with Gorgon's dark anger ringing in our ears.

*

I watched my aunt potter to and fro, seldom settling for more than a mouthful at a time as she saw to everyone's wants. Kind-hearted and scatter-brained, she was a storybook fairy-godmother, every bit as soft and affectionate as her mother had been strict and scolding.

I had spent the odd holiday with my aunt. 'Loaned out,' as my father put it. I got 'loaned out' to various relatives for the summer without the rest of the family, especially now I was old enough to be useful. I went, sometimes, to Joan's, or to my Gran's in Wales, or Aunt Bet in Surrey. It was a privilege not granted my brother and I guarded it carefully, never letting on how much I loved these trips lest I was prevented from going.

I cast my gaze over the 'bit of tea' that Aunt Joan had laid out. The huge table seated seven people that day, with room to spare. It was piled rim to rim with food. Cakes, like the luminescent sponge covered with peppermint icing, fluffed into wintery peaks deepening into rich leaf-green in the depths that lurked beneath; gold-brown coffee and walnut cake with pale brown icing forked into swirling ripples eddying out from the half-walnut placed ceremonially at its centre; dark, moist chocolate cake, one of the gooey kind, with searing red cherry halves perched uneasily around its edge in genuine danger of being swept away on the laval flow of shiny chocolate that dripped down the sides. Salad, ham, cheese, pickles, mustard, home made jam and lemon curd, jelly, even a blanc-mange. Great chunks of fresh, yeasty bread spread thick with butter.

And, of course – tea.

Aunt Joan's *Sunday Tea* could not be faulted by any countryman's standards, but her success in brewing the beverage itself could never be relied on in any fashion whatsoever, and it was her non-stop chatter that would often lend added bite to the end result.

Sometimes that big chocolate brown enamel teapot dispensed a deep red and bitter brew from sitting too long on the hob. On occasion it had been known for her to attempt a brew with cold water, having forgotten to boil the kettle at all.

I waited as the big tin pot was poised over the cups set in a friendly cluster near Aunt Joan's plate. Joan was still chattering as she poured. 'You know Billy? Alf's wife's youngest brother? Well ... he wrote to me last week, an' asked if he could visit. You could've knocked me over ... I haven't heard from young Billy for ... oh, it must be ten years if it's a day. I didn't know he knew where we lived to tell you the truth. Funny boy is Billy.'

She bubbled on, with my parents nodding, and murmuring at intervals. To try to speak would be pointless when Joan was in full flood.

'He never came round much after Alf was gone. Shame really, he could've done with company. Their mother wasn't an 'appy soul, what with losing her 'usband, as well as the eldest boy. Both in the Navy they were.'

I began to giggle as I watched the liquid cascading into the first cup. Joan did not notice at first, the steam having coated her glasses at the first splash. The liquid was hot, and yes, it was steaming ... and also crystal clear. Joan had forgotten to put the tea-leaves into the pot – again.

Cowslip or Primrose Wine

1 gall of cowslip flowers (yellow flower parts only; stalk, etc. makes a sour flavour)

3½ lb of loaf sugar

2 oranges

1 lemon

4 oz sultanas or raisins

1 gall of water (spring water if possible)

Method

1. Wash the flowers and place them in a crock.

2. Put water and sugar into a large pan and simmer until it is clear, skimming frequently. Pour this liquid over the flowers and stir in sultanas.

3. Cover the crock and leave for four days, stirring twice each day and then strain off the liquid into a fermentation jar with an air-lock and allow to ferment.

4. When the fermentation is complete bottle and store in racks for at least eight months.

5. When making cowslip wine please bear in mind that many flower species, such as cowslips, are a protected by law, and should never be picked from the wild. If you don't have this many cowslips in your own garden then obtain dried flowers from an herbalist. There are a great many flower wines to be made with this method.

6. For example: marigolds, roses, dandelions, daisies, wallflowers, honeysuckle, elder flowers and meadow sweet can all be used in place of cowslips. The list goes on, but if you are not sure on the toxicity of any flowers not named here ask an herbalist for advice before using them. Cowslips and primroses, for instance, should be avoided by pregnant

women; those on blood thinning drugs or those sensitive to aspirin.

Medicinal

Cowslips and Primroses collectively have been attributed with much the same properties. They are said to cure:

Flower (as a tea): headaches (especially migraine), fevers and chills; (as a tincture): insomnia and anxiety, as well as calming the nerves; (as a compress): facial ticks and neuralgia, rheumatic/ arthritic pain; (as an ointment): ringworm, sunburn and allergies; (essential oil in a bath): insomnia; (in a massage oil): for nerve pain and migraine.

Root parts (decoction or tincture): coughs, bronchitis measles, asthma and rheumatic/ arthritic pain.

Plus unspecified: a cure for jaundice.

Cowslip wine is thought to be especially good for insomnia.

Cowslips were also known as palsywort and were once used to cure palsy. Primroses boiled in lard was a well known cure for cuts, burns, scalds and sores in the south-coast counties.

Traditional

Cowslips – called the flowers of happiness – are said to have the power to split rocks containing treasure, and that fairies can be persuaded to give up gold for these flowers.

Cowslips are said to aid in finding lost treasure.

Many of the folklore attached to cowslips and primroses are linked to the fey folk, or Good Neighbours as they were often known. Country people were wary of the Queen-under-the-hill and her entourage. They would seldom mention fairies by name, and the euphemisms were always kindly in case the fey ones took offence and struck down either them or their crops and stock.

Planted upside down on Good Friday they were said to turn into primroses (or alternatively primroses planted upside down would grow red flowers).

Cowslips had an association with maypoles, which may hint at a sacrificial origin, yet at the same time they were used as an element in garlands to ward off witches.

Cowslips were regarded as a seasonal signal as many people insisted you would never get warm and settled weather until the paigles (cowslips) were finished flowering.

Girls made paigle-balls and tossed them in the air as they chanted *Tinker, tailor, soldier, sailor, rich man, poor man, beggar man, thief.* When the last flower fell out of the ball she would marry a man of that persuasion.

A woman who washed her face with milk infused with cowslip was thought to draw her beloved closer to her.

Cowslips were also believed to induce contact with departed loved ones during dreams, be a powerful healing agent, promote youthfulness.

Primroses – the February flowers – cousins to the cowslip were thought to be the key into the Kingdom-under-the-Hill and that eating primrose blossoms allowed a child to see fairies (I ate hundreds of primroses and cowslips as a child, sucking the nectar from the base of the petals – they are very sweet – but I never saw even one fairy; ah well).

Traditionally the first posy of primroses picked and brought into the house should never number less than fourteen; thirteen or less will bring bad luck in the hen-house and dictates the number of chicks hatched that spring.

Mead, Metheglin & Maypoles

The class had been practising for weeks, prancing in circles and clinging reluctantly to lengths of faded ribbon attached to the top of an old netball post. Later that day they would finally have the real thing, the rough-hewn Maypole, topped with its crown of flowers set in the edge of the village cricket and football grounds; the combined space which made up the nearest thing Haltwood had to a village green. For now they practiced with a grim determination.

I sat with Linda and watched the rest of the class trying to weave the braids into patterns, before retracing their steps to release it all once more. Back and fore; in and out. The taped music cut off abruptly as, yet again, the dancers had tied themselves into knots.

We could hear Mrs Evans scolding one of the Garton boys for 'fooling around'. We both groaned and tutted from our sideline position of absolute superiority. Linda maintained that had we been dancing all of this stopping and starting would, of course, have been unnecessary. We would do it right every time. She would have loved a chance to be amongst the Maypolers, but, along with half our classmates, we weren't needed. Being in the senior class was the worst for school events; being too big for the massed appearances put on by the infants, and too numerous for even half of us to have any kind of meaningful part to play. What it meant in practice was that those of us not pretty enough, or more likely not possessed of parents on the school board, were not chosen at all.

As I hated being in the public eye, and was basically lazy, I was not so unhappy. Linda, on the other hand, took her exclusion very personally. She sat on the edge of the field, picking fault with the proceedings wherever she could, whilst I did my utmost to humour her. I plucked a few more daisies to add to my chain, whilst Linda scowled deeply and darkly as she watched Mrs Evans disentangling Bob Fuller from a dozen strands of ribbon.

'Gurt great clod,' Linda muttered. 'Jest cos he's top in maths, an' 'is dad's on the council.' She glanced across the field to where the village Maypole stood, white and gleaming, ribbons of red and green and gold, and garlands of flowers dripped from the top with more heaped high around the base. Mr Hurst was nominally in charge of the Morris pole, and the village dancers who cavorted around it, though everybody knew that 'Goody' Hurst was the boss. The village Maypole had already been danced around at sunrise, and would be danced again when the sun set. Linda would always get a part when her Gran and Dad were in charge but she was not to be pacified in regard to the school's junior, and to her obviously inferior version.

'Them yafflers wouldn't be dancin' round the real pole if Gran had her say.'

'I know,' I said, trying to distract her from her moaning. 'I think its matching feet Bob needs most. The ones he's got keep going in different directions.' I watched the dancers, a smile twitching around my face. 'He's not the only one, mind. That Angela's not much better, no matter how many ribbons she'd got in 'er hair.'

'I'm bored,' Linda announced. 'Let's go see en put up the stalls.'

'Okay.' I agreed readily enough. This was a plus to being a spare part in school business. We had the chance to have a look round before the crowds arrived. I would have done the rounds already but an hour had been wasted waiting for Linda to get over her sulks.

We rose quietly and edged discreetly from the group, sneaking away like Cornish pirates with a *very* cat-like tread. May Day festivities were held on the nearest Saturday, though on that year the two coincided, and our presence was more expected than required. Slipping away without teachers seeing us still carried a certain frisson, not least because the rest of our class were being so very *good*.

The fete was due to open at two, and the field was abuzz with scurrying people rushing here and there with chairs and poles and battle-scarred trestle tables. Huge bundles of tired-looking bunting still waited in heaps to be strung between stalls. Rumour had it these 'community' streamers had been hand-sewn in anticipation not of the Queen's coronation but of her father, King George VI's. I could well believe it. In fact, judging by its appearance of genteel, faded, decrepitude they could well have dated back to Victoria's Jubilee. I did know it could all have done with a good wash, but I strongly suspect it would never have survived the process.

We stepped between these muted heaps and scuttled toward the fair ground section before the elderly Miss Bishop, the uncrowned bunting queen, could shanghai us into her work party.

Like the faded flags and streamers, the rides and stalls belonged to the village committee, and to a different era. Each of them was trundled out every year to be screwed and nailed into general working order; checking and repairing and repainting being as familiar as breathing to the usual suspects on the various committees.

There were the swing-boats and roundabouts and their pride and joy a tiny helter-skelter. Then there were side-shows like the ever-present coconut shy. Pitch and toss was a late summer stall, and the Young Farmers Guild had replaced it with welly-wanging. We had a greasy-pole contest, which was new and we paused to gaze at in delighted wonder. Its long central pole, suspended between mini wooden scaffolds, had been de-barked and painted in bright, primary stripes so that it resembled a long, unyielding, necklace. Beneath it a group of lads were rigging up a large tarpaulin, supported on straw bales to serve as the dunking pool.

'You gonna have a go, Sue?' Linda said.

I examined the rough pole carefully and shook my head. 'Nope. I don't want splinters in me bum.'

Linda giggled, glancing around to see if anyone had heard me using a naughty word. 'Mrs Evans should 'ave a go then. My ol' Dad calls her iron-knickers.'

We both giggled, leaning against each other for support. It was a weak joke, and we knew it, but with the Maypolers way behind us and so much fun in front, it was becoming one of those days when everything was hysterically funny.

We moved on, tittering quietly. There were still so many half-finished stalls that it was hard to imagine it was less than two hours before kick-off.

Most of the remaining attractions were housed in three marquees. It was in these canvas temples ruled by the W.I. that the village matrons, assisted by Guides, Scouts, Young Farmers Guild and other village stalwarts, would sell home made cakes and a variety of hand-made produce to the more unwary revellers.

We wandered around until we got under one pair of feet too many and were chased out toward the cricket pavilion, beyond which was the Beer Tent. That was out of bounds to us *maids*, but we could not resist creeping round to the side to peer under the flaps at a gloomy interior. It was disappointingly ordinary. A few tables and chairs were being set up with several long trestles at one end on which stood a number of barrels. We only got a brief glimpse before one of Linda's many uncles turned to wave a warning hand, shooing us away like mice at a corn fair. Beer tents back then did not welcome small girls.

We fled, crippled in fresh hysteria, past the cricket square that would see the Celebrity Cricket Match later in the day, and on down to the football pitch.

This was roped off for the Dog Show and already milling with early-arriving hounds and handlers. We stood watching them for some time.

'What d'ya reck'n on that then?' Linda muttered, pointing at a pink-beribboned toy poodle. 'Wouldn't give that'n much've a chance agin' some big ol' buck rat. He bain't no bigger than one to start with.'

I nodded. Both our fathers were proud of their respective dog's rat-catching prowess, and rated canines generally on that criterion. 'Looks like a rat-on-a-string,' I added.

The dog's owner bent to fasten a pink, fluffy, coat around the tiny dog, and we both turned away to hide our amusement. Our collie-dogs spent their lives out in the open, in all weathers and in every season, and neither of us could conceive of the notion of canine apparel. That was for posh dogs and wusses.

'Morning girls. Good joke?'

We turned guiltily and smiled at the retired head-teacher, Mr Fletcher. His face, peering over the hedge, was swathed in fine, black netting suspended around his head and shoulders from a wide brimmed hat.

We looked around, suddenly aware that we had walked a long way from the action, and were near the overgrown orchard garden where Mr Fletcher kept his half-dozen beehives. In our noisy chatter we had failed to notice the insects flitting around us, or the lazy hum of bees drowsing in the sunlight. He waved his smoke-can toward the hives.

'You're all right,' he beamed at them. 'I've been smoking them. They won't sting if you leave them be. I'm only extracting Honey-Combs from one,' he said, waving a lidded bucket at us. 'To sell on the produce stalls.' He beckoned us into the garden and handed over the lidded bucket. 'Take this up to the School House will you? And tell Mrs Fletcher I'll be up in a few minutes. I've got some errands for you to run.'

'Yes Sir.'

We hopped the orchard fence, took the bucket between us, and toiled up through rows of twisted and ancient fruit trees. A few sleepy bees whirred around our heads, following their missing provender. We both knew better than to wave them away. By the time we reached the back door all of the bees had left us to return to their violated hive.

I knocked tentatively on the open door, and called out,

'Mrs Fletcher? Hello? We got the honey bucket, and Mr Fletcher says we've to run an errand.'

'Oh, Susan… And Linda. An errand. Really?' She was flustered and flushed. 'Come in girls. Set that down in the pantry will you?' She motioned us toward the pantry door, and went back to her cakes. She was a round lady, as short as her husband was tall. The string of her apron cut her into a pair of spheres so that with her white blouse and snowy hair she resembled a plump, ruddy-faced, cottage loaf.

Mrs Fletcher was as well known for her gossip as her cakes. She was leaning, tongue peeping between her teeth, and lowering a cushion-like, sugar-crusted sponge cake onto a paper-doilied plate. Not a sound but the deep ticking of a large clock that stood somewhere in the house beyond the hallway door.

'There, she said. 'If that doesn't get a prize this year I don't know what will.'

When Mr Fletcher came into the kitchen he was humming to himself. He smiled at us as he hung his hat and bee-veil on the back of a chair. 'Not dancing this year?' he said. 'Well … never mind. You're both up to senior school next year. I expect your Gran will get you on the seniors' Morris team very soon, Linda. Got anything else to do right now?' He reached into a cupboard and pulled out a pair of stone flagons. 'I've got a job for you two. There's sixpence in it.'

I looked at Linda and nodded. Sixpence was worth having.

'What is it?' Linda said. 'We told my ma we wouldn't be long.'

'I'll tell her you're on an errand,' Mrs Fletcher said. 'I must get over to the W.I. judging tables now or I will miss it. She is there isn't she? Never mind … must dash.' She picked her precious cake and headed for the door. 'See you later girls.' She all but ran out of the door. Meanwhile Mr. Fletcher was waving the large flagons at us and grinning like the schoolboys that he had taught until just a year or two before.

'I've got to go over to the pavilion,' he said. 'Take these

over to Doctor Batchelor, will you?'

'Won't he be there?' I asked. 'He's on the cricket eleven today isn't he?'

'He is. But he's helping put up the swing boats and these are – important.'

I took a flagon from him and examined it doubtfully. I had seen enough similar jars to wonder why these had such apparent value. 'Cider?' I said. 'But there'll be plenty in the beer tent won't there.'

'Not cider, child. Metheglin. And this...' he thrust the second flagon at Linda, '...is mead. My own brew. The final two from last year's batches. So don't fall over and break them.' He shoved a sixpence in my free hand. 'Off you go, quick now. And one more thing.' He raised a finger to his lips. 'Not a word to anyone. Our secret. Okay?'

'Yes Mr Fletcher, I mean no, Mr Fletcher.' I sidled toward the door, eager to get this over as quickly as possible. Beyond the hall door the clock boomed out twelve strokes.

'My mam'll be lookin' fer us,' said Linda. 'We'd better shift us selves.' She hurried me out, pulling the door closed behind us. 'Mam says we can have a sandwich from the tea tent,' she declared proudly, 'cos she didn't have time to make nothin' before.'

Most matrons of the village saw shop-bought sandwiches as profligate, and to buy them a slur on a woman's prowess on a par in the sinful stakes with backless party-frocks and the demon drink. My own mother's sole concession to 'shop-bought' was the occasional slab of Angel-Cake from the Woolworth's counter in Horsham. I, on the other hand, saw shop bought anything as a treat to be savoured. With that lure of 'shop bought' large in my mind, we jogged up the field to seek out Dr Batchelor.

'Mr Fletcher sent these, and said en were a secret,' Linda announced as she handed her flagon over.

The doctor twitched the jars away from us and stowed them rapidly under the edge of the ride, glancing both ways to see who may have seen the transaction.

Linda, ever the opportunist, saw her chance. 'Why're they secret then?' she asked loudly.

He stared down at her a mix of horror flitting around his gaunt features. 'They just are,' he replied. A stock answer and Linda, began to subside, realising there was no other answer to be had, and then, 'But...'

'Here.' The doctor thrust a sixpence into her hand. 'Secrets are secrets. If I told you then it wouldn't be one. Now get yourself an ice cream and forget about it.' Taking another quick glance around him he sneaked the flagons back from where we had left them and skulked off toward his car.

Linda pocketed her additional earnings and grinned at me. 'Don't know what they be on at,' she said. 'An' I don't care. Guilt. It never fails. Come on. Time we got somethin' to eat.'

We ran back to the marquee and the W.I. cake stall where Linda's mother was wrapping crepe paper around the leg of a trestle table.

'You've bin a while,' she said, rising slowly to her feet, and pushing honey-blonde hair from her face. 'Your mum went home, Susan. She said she had lambs' feed-bottles to mix.'

I nodded emphatically. 'We helped Mr Fletcher with an errand.' I beamed at Mrs Hurst, wanting, as always, to bask in her approval. She was not the typical countrywoman, though she had lived in Haltwood all her life. I felt she looked more like a film star with her petite figure and fragile features. She was a parson's daughter, with an education. She made clay pots and wove rugs rather than the jam or cakes that her neighbours produced for the show. She was often whispered to have 'married beneath her' though back then I never understood quite what that implied. In my eyes Virginia Hurst was perfect. Did it matter if she could not make a fluffy sponge, or a well-dispersed jar of strawberry jam? Not when she could throw clay on a wheel and make wonderful pots and vases and plates, or weave glittering pictures in wool and cotton yarn.

I waited as Mrs Hurst produced a crinkled ten-shilling note from her purse and handed it to Linda. 'Go and get your dinner girls. Bring it back here, and you can help me finish off this stall.'

By the time we had brought back cheese and pickle sandwiches, orange squash and cake, the stall was almost done and the cricket match already started.

'Can we go'n watch, mum?' Linda asked.

'Mrs Hurst said we were to help, but...' I held my breath.

She only laughed. 'Go on then, the pair of you. Be back by four.'

We needed no second telling, and ran out toward the cricket field before any minds were changed. The match had started before the Mayday fete's official opening and there was already a sprinkling of people watching.

It was than that we noticed Dr Batchelor's daughter, Lizzie, sitting all alone on the boundary line. We had joined her, and started our lunch, before we noticed that all was not well with village cricket.

As the bowler from the village team took his run up, the celebrity-batsman bent to the crease. A movement just to the right of the batsman attracted the girls' attention. A large hairy retriever half-rose, tense and expectant; its long tongue flopped from a jowly mouth that drooled glutinous strands of saliva as she panted heavily.

The batsman waved his bat at the dog, but it only gulped at the saliva ropes and wagged a well-plumed and ingratiating tail.

Linda sniggered quietly. 'That's Sally your dog isn't it, Lizzie?' she said.

Lizzie nodded, shrinking down, pulling her jumper up over her nose, to hide her face, and peeping over the neck band like a tousle-haired Chad. 'Clunking big fool,' she hissed. 'What's she doing yoysterin' about like that?'

'You goin' to call her?' I asked.

I was rewarded with a withering glance. 'Not likely. Bad enough the locals knowing it's mine, let alone go out there and fetch her back.' She peered around her, wondering how many people had seen us. The umpire, Tim Ralph, looked in our direction and half nodded. Yet, far from seeming annoyed, I noted a half smile on his face before he turned back to the game. Lizzie groaned again, closing her eyes, and only opened them once more, surprised when the expected summons did not come.

The ball left the bowler's fingers in a smooth arc toward the wicket. The batsman bent a little lower, his gaze fixed on the ball. Mr Ralph took a step left to view the ball from a better angle; and Sally hauled her eight stone frame onto soup-plate paws in readiness.

Leather and wood came together with a blow that echoed around the entire field. It was a good slog that sailed over the fielders and bounced toward the boundary where Len was fielding. I watched him leaping after the ball, sweeping it up in a rolling arc and flinging it back toward the wicket. This was his first match with the village team, and he was enjoying every moment.

The batsman left his crease, bat held before him like a grail, and ran toward the far wicket – and Sally came too. She bounced along the length of the wicket with her curious rocking-horse gait, red-flag tongue flapping in the wind, ears up and tail high. She did not touch the runner, but ran close to his legs, her head turned toward him in question just ahead of his pad-impeded knee. From the other direction the other batter was forced into a wide path to avoid the flailing tail attached to Sally's ample rear end.

The ball that had left Len's hand a second ago was caught by the bowler and whacked into the stumps moments before the batsman's desperate lunge for the crease.

'Out!' Mr Ralph shouted.

The batsman scowled at the dog, and began to argue the point. The umpire pointed toward the pavilion, without another word. The batsman trailed off to cool his temper and was replaced by another visitor; who gave Sally a long meaningful stare, hefting his bat as he took his place before the stumps.

The bowler took his run-up. The batsman flicked his bat at Sally. Unperturbed, Sally moved a few feet away, and watched him eagerly. Leather rocketed against willow. The batsman took a few paces toward her, almost colliding with a fielder who was attempting to sneak a rear-guard action on the canine infiltrator. Sally side-stepped him, galumphing around the two of them in her heavy-boned version of frisky skips. They both tried another grab but, despite her bulk, she evaded capture, bouncing a few feet further on, and turning to gaze at them with bright eyed anticipation. The celebrities tried bribery, calling to her in wheedling tones, but she was having none of it and danced away, her exertions becoming quicker as her excitement grew. It was obvious to all that she was having a wonderful game, even if the visiting team were not. The players grabbed for her several times, but at each attempt she ran just fast enough to avoid their grasping hands.

Disgusted they returned to the creases, and Sally bounced back to her spot just beyond the batsman's reach.

The bowler took his next run, sending a low shot to the crease, and the batsman took it greedily, sending the ball howling toward the boundary. He ran, and Sally ran, and the fielders ran. The ball was snatched up just short of the boundary. It flew from the fielder's hand, found the bowler, and continued, into the wicket a second before the batsman sprawled into the crease in a tumbling heap. Sally yelped as his bat managed to clip her padded bum; but still the bails flew across the grass as a hail of laughter and clapping hands acknowledged the umpire's raised finger.

'Out!' The call echoed across the field, and the batsman turned to glare at him. His mouth opened and shut a few times as he floundered for the right words.

Both teams milled around for a few seconds, and then Mr

Ralph shouted out. 'Y'ere, Lizzie. Come an' get your ol' dog will you?'

She shrank back behind Linda and me, but the village team captain, Barry Charman, was already striding toward her. As he reached us I could see he was grinning broadly. 'Lizzie Batchelor,' he said, in an overloud and theatrical tone, 'your ol' dog's a cursed nuisance, getting' under folks feet. Come an' take 'er 'ome will you?' As he stood in front of us his right eye closed in a slow wink.

Lizzie stared back at him, and then struggled to her feet. 'C'mon Sal,' she shouted. 'Come here.'

Sally lolloped across the field with every part of her, from tongue to tail, flopping and drooping with the effort. I held out the remains of a sandwich, and as Sally took it, Lizzie fumbled in the dog's thick coat for her chain collar.

'Thanks. We're in bat soon,' said Barry, and he gave us another slow wink as he turned back onto the field.

'You know what this means doncha Lizzie?' Linda giggled. 'I think your Sal's gone an' won us the cup.'

Lizzie nodded gloomily. 'Yes, but my father will go mad. I was supposed to tie her up in the back garden before I come out.'

'But your old dad's out there,' I said, nodding toward the retiring fielders.

'I know ... oh I know! He will be mad.'

'No ee won't,' Linda said. She eyes the doctor speculatively. 'I got a feelin' your old Pa knows a lot more than he's lettin' on at. He's grinning like a badger. If'n he'd wanted your Sal orf the field, 'ed've got her hisself. Nah. Take my word, Lizzie. Your dad's 'appy as a pig.'

'She's right you know.' I put a comforting arm around her shoulders. 'He'll be so glad the team's winning he won't care.'

Lizzie sniffed in disgust, tugging Sally away toward the stalls. 'Yes. And there go the flying pigs,' she grumbled. 'Come on you flea-ridden baggage.' She tugged hard at

Sally's choke chain. 'You and your tricks will get me shot.' She limped away toward the Hall on calliper-ridden feet, a legacy of the last polio epidemic, hauling Sally behind her. The dog, knowing that she was somehow in disgrace, plodded heavily behind her with ears back and tail low.

We followed them slowly up the field. And as we walked people were smiling at the dog. Comments of 'Good girl, Sal' and 'does Freddie Truman know 'bout 'er?' came from all sides. Sally was pummelled and patted, and was holding head and tail high when they reached the cake stall.

'What have you two been doing?' Mrs Hurst demanded. 'I've been having people saying all kinds of things.'

'It's not Linda's fault, Mrs Hurst,' I said quickly. 'We was helping Lizzie Batchelor with her dog. Sally was running with the batsmen an' they got cross with her. But Barry never said nothin' till it was our turn'n in, and then he got us to take her away. So we had to bring her here.'

Mrs Hurst stared at us for a few moments. Her eyes sparkled, and her lips twitched, so that I was sure she was going to laugh. 'Lizzie, didn't your Dad tie her up?' she asked finally.

Lizzie's head drooped into her chest. 'I don't know Mrs Hurst,' she mumbled. 'I was sure she couldn't get out when I left home.'

'Maybe so, but we can't have her clumping around the cakes all afternoon. That dog eats like three horses. And you can't walk all that way either, Lizzie. You'll have to find your brother, and tell him I said to take Sally home.'

Lizzie sighed and looked at me for help. Her elder brother, Jack, would not be happy leaving the fair early. And though she would do as she was told we knew that Lizzie would suffer for it in some dire fashion.

Linda and I moved a little closer, surreptitiously twining fingers with Lizzie's in a silent vote of support. Her glance twitching toward us in equally mute thanks.

'We won, Mrs Hurst,' I said, not sure if wheedling would

have any effect. It didn't work on my own mother but my father was a frequent victim so it was worth a try. 'We haven't won the cricket cup for five years, and Sally won it. Honest.'

'Can't we just find some string'n take Sally with us til it's time?' Linda added. 'She didn't mean to do nothin' wrong. Not really. She were only yoysterin'. Please Mum?'

'An' Lizzie didn't do nothing wrong,' I was getting anxious for our friend, and incensed at the blame she was taking for her elder siblings. 'It's not fair if she has to go home just cos...'

Mrs Hurst held up her hand for quiet. 'So you think that 'Fair is foul, and *fowl* is fair?' She asked.

'Hover through the fog and filthy air.' Mrs Fletcher rose from where she had been kneeling at the other end of the table and began to laugh.

To our relief Mrs Hurst joined in. We had no idea what they were talking about, but we laughed anyway, nudging Lizzie to do likewise. Where adults were concerned we worked on a general rule of public co-operation, and found it gained us ground in most instances. The two women spent a lot of time saying strange things of the kind and found it hilarious, so it seemed a good plan to join in.

'I tell you what,' Mrs Fletcher said, finally. 'Seeing as Charlotte has taken our donkey to give rides this afternoon, we'll put Sally in the stable until it's time to go home. Is that all right, Virginia?' she favoured Linda's mother with a wry smile. 'I don't think even Sally can knock that door down.'

'If you're sure it's no trouble, Julia?'

'No trouble. I have to go and get some more drawing pins anyway. Come on girls. We'll put that rogue Sally in a safe place and then you can help finish this crepe paper for me.'

We looked at each other for silent confirmation. We'd already been landed with a lot of chores today, but it was better than walking two miles to Lizzie's home, and a million times better than earning a place in Jackie's bad graces.

'And,' as Linda later observed, 'we knows secrets and

stuff. Dursn't we?'

*

The stables lay just to the rear of the schoolhouse on the path that led straight into the orchard; where the Fletcher's old donkey, Theodore, kept both grass and windfall fruit to a minimum, aided and abetted by two brown goats, Tina and Minty.

As we reached the rear of the schoolhouse Mrs Fletcher paused frowning first at the open door, and then at us two girls. 'Did you shut that when you came out?' she demanded.

'Yes,' said Linda.

'But we didn't have no keys to lock it with,' I added.

'We didn't have *a* key,' she corrected me, absently. 'I know your mother taught you better grammar than that.' She advanced on the door and reached out to shut it properly, but as she stretched for the handle it was torn from her grasp.

A man barged through the opened doorway, sending Linda crashing into Mrs Fletcher's sprawling herb patch. Sally's makeshift lead slipped from her grasp and the dog was off, gambolling down the path after this latest playmate.

'Linda, go for help,' Mrs Fletcher shouted before she broke into a running pursuit, and I was hot on her heels.

The intruder was almost at to the end of the orchard, and Sally was still cavorting around his legs. He lashed out at her with a brown canvas holdall, trying to strike her head, but Sally was having fun. She darted back from the blow, and dived in once more, uttering deep gruffing sounds that were as close as she ever came to a bark.

He swung again.

'Stop. Stand still or I shall order her to attack,' Mrs Fletcher shouted.

I came to a halt, standing a few feet behind the adult, and stared at her. Sally. I was fairly sure, would never know how to attack anything; if you discounted her supper.

Sally herself took full advantage of this lull and with supreme effort raised herself onto her hind legs, like some lumbering, blonde, bear, to grab at the bag. Her huge jaws closed around one of the handles and she crashed back to earth. Gravity took hold of the dog's considerable mass and carried both bag and burglar with her to landfall.

The intruder released the carry-all, and launched himself away from the dog, screeching all the while for us to, 'Get it off. Help. Get this bloody dog off've me.'

As he fell his head struck a squat white hive nestling beneath a greengage tree, scattering its various sections in all directions. There was a silence that lasted for what could only have been a bare second before the bees rose from the carnage in an angry cloud.

I whistled to Sally and retreated up the path, followed by Linda and Mrs Fletcher. The intruder was only a pace or two behind us, but was hampered by bees careening around him like a dark cloud.

The insects fell away rapidly; more intent on saving the queen once the attacker was in retreat but the running procession reached the stable before we halted.

By now a crowd had gathered in the garden in answer to Linda's screeching pleas for help with Roland Dyer, the village policeman, foremost among them. A staunch member of the team he seldom missed a match, but he was also seldom off duty.

He dodged forward to grab the man's arm, assisted by Jimmy Shotter. 'You all right Julia?' he asked Mrs. Fletcher.

'I am fine, thank you for asking, Dyer.' She watched, exasperated, as her husband rushed past her without a word, his head swathed in his netted hat, to check his precious hives. 'I think Sally did very well.' She ran quickly through the tale and ended with a dour look at me. 'You should not have followed me young lady, it could have been dangerous.'

'Sally was very brave,' I replied. 'She stopped him didn't he?'

'She did. I never knew the old girl had it in her.'

'Always got some energy where her stomach's concerned,' her husband replied as he reappeared with the holdall. 'I will have to leave the hives for now. They're far too annoyed to move yet. But I've got the bag.' He grinned suddenly. 'I think Sally is more interested in cake breaking than crime busting.' He opened the bag, and took out a couple of tarts. 'I rather think she was after these.' He looked at the dog sitting to attention, looking expectantly at the cake in his hand. 'But I can't begrudge her.' He reached and took out the silver trophy. 'Seems she's saved the cup in all ways.'

Mead

2-3 lb of honey (depending on taste)

1 oz of fresh yeast

1 oz of dried hops

2 gall of water

1 slice of toast

Method

1. Good mead takes time, so expect to wait for this one.
2. Put the hops and honey into the water and boil slowly for an hour.
3. Cool to lukewarm, and then place in a crock.
4. Spread yeast onto the toast and float on the top.
5. Cover the crock and leave for four days.
6. Strain and pour the liquid into a fermentation jar with a lock.
7. Bottle after one year and store for at least one further year.

Melomel (fruit mead)

In addition to the above ingredients, use approximately two pounds of rosehips, boiled, mashed and strained through muslin.

Then use the same method as for mead.

Vary amounts of fruit and honey according to taste.

Metheglin (spiced mead)

4 lb of honey

1 oz of hops

½ oz of root ginger

2 cloves

¼ oz of cinnamon bark or eight ounces of caraway seed

Method

1. Use the same method as for mead.

2. You can use other flavourings such as mace, marjoram, lemon, balm etc. but use them sparingly.

Medicinal (honey)

To list the properties given to honey would take a whole book on its own, so I will just list a few: sedative, antibacterial (internal and external), anti-fungal (internal and external), bruises, burns, cuts, hay fever, ringworm, nappy rash, gargle, eye wash, cough remedy, face mask and arthritis/ rheumatism.

Take honey mixed with cider vinegar in hot water to reduce problems such as hay fever, hangovers, caffeine headaches etc.

Bees were also made to sting swollen joints to ease the inflammations.

As with all wine recipes I cannot say that fermented items have the same curative powers, but if it does, then mead has to be one of the most pleasant tasting medicines available.

Traditional (honey)

Also the rhyme below is well known.

> *A swarm of bees in May is worth of load of hay.*
> *A swarm of bees in June is worth a silver spoon.*
> *A swarm of bees in July isn't worth a fly.*

The later in the season bees swarm the less time they have to gather sufficient food for the winter.

It was said that bees would never stay with a bad-tempered keeper, and traditionally a keeper will never swear in front of his bees; certainly bees react to the tone of the human voice.

In Sussex, there was a custom of bee-wassailing on Twelfth Night to ensure the well-being of the bees and their continued honey production for the year.

Oak leaves & Hand-Grenades

There were too many adult tempers that year frayed over spoiled hay and rain-beaten crops to give anyone an easy time. We had been kicking our heels for most of the week, lolling around in barns and woodlands, maintaining a low profile while waiting for the weather to improve.

Keeping occupied, however, was not easy when so many things were 'out-of-bounds'. Races to climb the outside of the Dutch barn, for instance, had been quite specifically banned since Roger Bennett had fallen off and broken his collar bone. Making tunnels in the bale-stacks left over from last year's harvest had a similar embargo, and the stream being in spate ruled out damming the shallows with rocks, grass-clods and handfuls of sticky blue and red clay.

So we sat in the Sussex Barn weaving baler twine into huge lengths of rope thick enough to take our weight as make-shift swings. Len's friend, Francis, was adamant that it be strung from a large horse chestnut tree that bordered the withy beds, while Linda and I favoured a temporary site here in the barn, slung from the rafters, with a nice soft hay landing if we fell off.

'Cissy stuff,' Len said. 'Anyway, Dad'll only make us take it down again.'

'Well then we c'n put it up somewhere else if he does,' I said, making Francis laugh.

'You look weird,' he tittered. 'Like the gargoyles on the chateau.'

I looked at Linda, who shrugged. 'He's one to talk,' she said.

To our Sussex ears Francis was a bit too posh; or rather he was a lot too posh. He lived at Dranton Manor on the far side of the canal, and went to some toff's school miles away, only coming home for weekends and holidays. Holidays which came about a lot earlier and lasted far longer than the state schools, much to our disgust.

Francis was a tall, gangly lad, a year older than Len, and more worldly-wise than any of us, with all his foreign words and high living. I cannot recall how he and Len had met, living such vastly different lives as they did, but they had been friends for years. I did like him, however. He was kind hearted and generous, and that made him a cut above most of the boys I knew, yet the gargoyle reference was uncalled for in my book. I scowled at him, and poked out my tongue.

'So what,' I said. 'I don't care what I look like. Least I'm not a talking 'cyclapedia.'

'S'roight,' Linda added. 'Lord Snooty.'

Francis, always affable, laughed and shook his head. 'Lord Snooty's the gang leader, so you'll have to do what you're told, chocolate-chops.

'I'm not.' I wiped my hand across my lips hurriedly, just in case he was right, and found that I did indeed have melted rainbow drops smeared over my mouth. I scrubbed surreptitiously at the sticky debris with my sleeve, and rammed the tattered packet into my trouser pocket, before returning to my wrapping of yellow strands of twine. The ends tangled for the umpteenth time, and I tugged angrily at the knotted mess. 'I'm bored with plating,' I said. 'We've gotta have something else we can do.'

Len looked at Francis and grinned. 'Fishing?' he said, slyly, knowing Linda would say no.

'That's not nice, poor fishes 'bain't got no chance,' Linda snorted.

'You eat lambs,' he replied.

'Mebbe, but leastways the butcher don't dangle lambs on a hook for ten minutes before he kills en.'

'No. He puts a gun on 'is head'n shoots the bugger's bloody brains out,' Len glanced at me, triumphant at my shocked face.

'Len,' I breathed, my hand clasped across my mouth,

accenting shock. 'You shouldn't cuss ... I'm tellin'.'

'You bain't, scraggy neck. Cos I'll tell Mum you used half your collection money last week for your seaside trip, an' stealin' off Sunday School's a lot worse than cussing.'

'Wasn't stealin',' I said. 'I was borrowin' it cos. Miss Meehan said we 'ad to 'ave our money in for the outing, an' I only had sixpence left out've my pocket money. Tersn't my fault I don't get as much as you do. Tersn't fair any how.'

Len frowned at me, glancing at Francis. 'I don't get none. Not now I got the Sat'day job.' He snapped. 'So there.'

I scowled, but said nothing more. Pay-parity in the pocket money stakes was always a bone of contention. I could not see even then why age and gender made such a difference to the amounts we were apportioned. I also hated the way in which Len tried to be so grand in front of his posh pal. So far as I was concerned money was a bit like having red-hair; some people had it, others didn't. The Birches were just a have-not-got sort of family. I knew life would be a lot more comfortable if we were a 'have' family; but we were have-not's and that was the end of it.

The knot suddenly capitulated under my angry onslaught. I shook out the gleaming length in triumph and tied off the ends, standing to stretch my share of the rope across the dusty floor in a glistening, if lumpy, golden serpent. 'That's got to be enough,' I shouted. 'Let's go put it up!'

The path through the withy beds was overgrown. Few people came here now that willow was no longer used. Coppiced stands curved up in thin, whippy strands. Polled ancients crouched with quivering wands rising from their stubby trunks; cut off in their prime to provide stakes and withy ties and still the bright green fronds of willow stretched and arched in all directions; ready and waiting for those weavers who no longer came.

Len and Francis strode ahead, shoving past the brambles and nettles along the whapple-way that trailed through the withies. As we walked, the bright shiny ramsons under-foot released their pungent garlicky smell.

I bent to pick a stem of slender-petalled flowers. I loved these starry little florets, searing white, with tiny black dots at their centres, though I wished they did not smell as strong so that I could take some home to put in a vase. Mother wouldn't allow them in the house; I knew that because I'd tried often enough. I let the flower drop to the ground as I realised I was falling behind the others.

Len marched at the head of the line, hefting the length of rope in one hand. Linda and I trotted along to the rear, excited, and nervous. This was forbidden territory strictly out-of-bounds without an adult when the River Arun was rising so far up the banks.

We still hadn't found a tree that suited both boys, though they had tried to lasso quite a number. Finding one with just the right branch at just the right height was not the simple task any of us had anticipated.

As we walked I glimpsed tantalising snaps of the river beyond the withy beds and shuddered. The surface boiled and twisted in pale chocolate-coloured strands; impenetrable and mystery-filled with who knew what lurking beneath that grasping expanse. I paused to watch a large branch, or perhaps it was a small tree, dipping among the ripples, wobbling into the air for a few seconds and then diving, sucked down into the fast flowing depths. It brought to mind a TV programme about dolphins I had seen, which showed the sea mammals rising and dipping in that very same way. But that was dolphins, and they did it on purpose. This was not the sea but a river. That swooping shape was an inanimate trunk being dragged out of view by forces I did not like to imagine. And wasn't wood supposed to float? I shuddered again, forcing my imagination to relinquish its hold. 'Can't we use the tree up on the ditch?' I called.

Len glanced at Francis, hopefully. Despite his bravado I could see he was not as immune to the latent threat of the swollen Arun as he would like the rest to think. 'We'd better,' he said. 'I'll only cop it off Mum if dim-bat there falls in.' He jerked a thumb toward me.

I poked out my tongue, retreating from the bank in case it turned out to be an argument I actually won.

Francis nodded. 'There's a good oak a bit further on that way.'

The boys backtracked a few yards and climbed the slope away from the roiling water, and I sighed with inward relief. I didn't like the deep water of the River Arun with its muddy water that concealed so much. Whether in spate or not it possessed a predatory presence that disturbed me for reasons I could never fathom. I was not bothered about the River Lox, even when it burst its banks and, on one occasion, swept the footbridge away on its brown expanse. The Lox was friendly water, but the Arun ... not so much. Lost once again in dark trails thoughts I was the last to reach the rise.

'Come on dolly-daydream,' Len shouted. He and Francis were already throwing the rope up to an outward branch of an oak tree leaning from the hedge.

'Nearly.' Linda was excited now.

I wondered if Linda had similar thoughts on the riverbank. It was likely as she seemed as reluctant to get close to the bank as I was. Only Francis seemed unaffected by the river's menace. But then he never seemed to worry over anything. He was possessed of a supreme confidence that bordered on the imbecilic. Nothing frightened him. Nothing worried him, even when he knew the punishment if he were caught.

I puffed to a halt next to Linda and joined in the taunting as the boys persisted in their abortive attempts to lasso the branch.

'Rope bain't long enough,' Linda shouted. ''Tis too high.'

Francis paused, staring up into dark-green leaves. He nodded. 'I think you're right, Lin. We need something a bit lower down.'

'Top barns are empty. So long as we take it down after, we could use the rafters on the stalls' end,' Len said.

Francis glanced up at a greying sky. 'Makes sense. It's going to tip down any minute,' he said, gathering up the rope in his long arms to lead us off toward the barns.

A few hundred yards further on the bank opened into a small plateau freshly scoured by the recent floods. The bank's lush grasses that normally covered the area were sprawled in a rank, brown mess of stalks criss-crossing the area in a sad mosaic. The area had been cleared by the floodwater as if swept by a huge yard-broom. Shallow rooted defences clinging to a meagre layer of soils had been whipped away, exposing an apron of cracked concrete and a brick wall along which were four evenly spaced slots; though all but one were clogged with detritus. At the left end of the wall a flight of steps led downwards to a doorway.

Len and Francis darted forward. Clambering down to what seemed to be a dead end from my viewpoint. The lads turned right and took more cautious paces forward.

I stood with Linda at the stair-head and we clutched each other in awed silence for several moments. The smell rising up toward us was rank and acrid with the odours of rotted vegetation and stagnant mud. It was dark. It was dank. It was everything every adventure book I had ever read warned me to avoid.

'What'cha reck'n then?' Linda murmured, finally.

'Not a lot,' I wrinkled my nose and frowned. Mud I could cope with and water was fine but that smell foretold to me everything that was bad. 'We could go just to the bottom. Just to look-see.'

'Right'o,' Linda started down, pulling me behind her.

I did not want to go any further into the dragon's lair. Normally I would have been hard on Len's heels, but instinct told me not to be comfortable with this place. It set alarms ringing and I had already begun to learn how to trust my inner siren.

It was easy to see what we were entering. We had all watched enough war films on telly, and seen plenty of pillboxes littering the countryside, to know the purpose of these dug-outs; leftovers from wartime defence plans that had never been used. Usually they were above ground, and invariably locked, being used by farmers as stores for feed or fertiliser.

This was different. This was a dark hole next to a river I did not trust. And furthermore one that had appeared out of nowhere. How often had we had passed this spot so many times and never gained a hint of this bunker's presence; dozens, maybe hundreds. It I did not think of myself as a coward, I enjoyed a challenge, but this seemed like tempting fate.

Len and Francis were already sloshing around in the gloom, calling dares and snips of sundry bravado at each other.

I took a deep breath as we paused by the opening, gagging slightly at the stench. The interior was dark, barely lit by the feeble light that filtered through the gun-slot and door. The foot of mucky water that covered the floor was the major source of the evil smell, releasing additional clouds every time the boys churned the depths with their welly booted feet.

'Tersn't nice,' Linda observed. 'I wouldn't be so wondered if you lads didn't catch the plague in there. 'Appen there be bodies in that-they water,' she said, and I giggled. Linda was always one with a gruesome notion lurking an inch or two below the surface of her 'curly-haired little angel' disguise. 'All bones ee'd be,' she added. 'No eyeballs left, even. Just skulls'n bones.'

'Shuddup,' Len sneered. 'You're all mouth, you are.'

'Yeah, an' you're all slugs and snails.' She replied. 'Slimy stuff. All goo'n'poo.' We leaned against each other laughing at her 'daring' words. The boys ignored us, refusing to be drawn.

As our eyes grew accustomed to the gloom we could see that the space was basically, and disappointingly, empty; devoid of all but a few boxes poking above the surface in the darker recesses. Some were of rusted metal, others broken lengths of wood and all saturated from the rising and ebbing of the river over the fourteen years since the bunker's desertion. They were a sorry collection.

Francis picked the nearest metal box from the water and dumped it on a wide concrete shelf that ran along the back wall. 'This one's still shut,' he said. 'It'll open if I get the rust off the seals.' He took out his penknife and began scraping around the edge of the box. Then, finally, the wire clip on its front slipped up and over clear of its anchor-point, and the lid lifted. He peered into it and uttered a yip of surprise.

With curiosity peaked, Linda and I edged into the bunker.

'Well?' Linda demanded after a full five seconds of silence. 'What's in it then?'

'Water,' Francis replied. He tipped the box carefully to one side, letting a stream of rusty liquid flow from it. And then a fist sized object slid to the edge of the lip, hovered there a moment as water rushed around it, and plopped into the murky floodwater before either Francis or Len could catch it. 'Damn.' He let the box sit back on its base and joined Len in grovelling in the silt around their feet.

'Got it,' Len held a lumpy object out for all to see. Rusted and covered in muck it was hard to tell what it might be. He stooped once more to swill it in the water, rising again to examine it more closely.

A pineapple-shaped metal lumps with a small handle on the top end where leaves would have been. We had all seen a 'million' of them on war films. It was unmistakable.

'Bloody hell,' Francis took it gingerly and moved to the open slit for better light. 'Bloody hell,' he repeated. 'No pin.'

'What?' Linda asked. 'What's a pin for?'

'It stops it blowing up. I think it must've rusted away.'

Linda laughed sharply. 'Yeah. Pull the other one. You and your daft jokes.'

'Who's joking?' he replied. 'This is a hand-grenade ... and the pin's missing.'

'And 'ow come you such an expert?' she snapped.

'Because, Miss Clever-Clogs, we have to go to cadets at my school. And we have to learn about this stuff.'

Linda and I glanced at one another, each trying to decide if the other thought this one Francis's elaborate hoaxes.

Francis himself was moving cautiously to the shelf with the exaggerated stealth of a pantomime comic. He laid the weapon carefully into the box once more and stumbled a few paces backwards.

Not a word was said, yet each of us reached the same conclusion at the same moment. Without warning Francis turned to run, gathering speed despite the hampering effects of mud and water.

We girls were ahead of him and were lurching up the steps almost before his hand had left the object and were out and across the field toward the top barns before the boys, both older and longer in the leg, had surged ahead. Being true gentlemen they came stomping past us as fast as their mud-caked wellies permitted and soon left us trailing in their wake. Never mind the rain that had started to fall whilst we had been underground. This was a case where every man, or woman, fended for themselves. The only thought on any of our minds right then was to put as much distance between us and the bunker as we possibly could.

We reached the top barns and piled into the storerooms, hurling ourselves among the remnants of last year's hay. We were laughing now, a mild hysteria lending an edge to its volume.

'Bugger, bwoy,' Linda punched Francis on the arm. 'You should've seen your face. It were a treat.'

He punched her back. 'Well, I couldn't see yours. You were running too fast.'

'Too roight I were. I wer'sn't staying around that thing. I bain't so green as cabbage lookin'.'

I sat up, picking hay from my hair and trying hard to stop the giggles. 'You think it really was one of them grenades? I mean, you only 'ad a little look.'

He nodded. 'Sure I'm sure.'

'Could've been a rock.'

He shook his head. 'Nope. That was definitely a grenade body. I've seen them before. Of course it may never have been primed.'

'What's 'at mean then?' Linda demanded.

'Firing pin might never have ever been fitted,' he replied. 'They get stored like that. In which case it was actually pretty safe.'

'But you don't know that,' said Len. 'It might've been a live one, only rusted bad. Or it might've been a dud in the first place.'

Francis laughed shortly. 'I wasn't about to look too hard. You can go back and check if you like.'

'No, ta,' said Len, 'I'll take your word for it.' He scrambled over to the window and rubbed a hole in the dust to look out. 'Still rainin',' he added. 'Wanna make that swing rope still?'

'One of us will have to go back for the rope,' said Francis. He glanced at his watch and frowned. 'Oh damn and blast. It's gone three already. Tomorrow maybe? I really have to be home on time today. Mater has some god-awful aunts coming for tea and she left orders. I have to be there; clean a combed and ready for inspection. You know what these old dears can be like.'

We all nodded our sympathy, though not so much that we would take the duty of rope retrieval on ourselves.

'Bad luck,' I muttered. 'We'll have to go an' all. We'd better go back and find you a mac, Linda, cos you've gotta get home all the way across the common in this rain.'

We trooped back out into the lane, going in the same direction for a few more yards at least.

''Ere, Len, d'ya think we should tell Dad?' I asked. ''Bout that bunker thing?'

He stopped dead, and turned, pointing a mud streaked

finger into my face. 'You dare. We'd bain't meant to go down the withies. 'Specially in this sort of weather. Mum'll go bananas.'

'S'pose so. But what if someone else finds it, en it goes orf?'

'I'll tell my father,' Francis replied. 'He's still in the reserves. He'll get some of his cronies out to have a look.'

'But then we won't get to go back there. They'll board it all up,' Linda complained.

'Makes no mind t'me. I bain't goin' down there again,' I replied. 'You can, if you loike. I bain't goin' nowhere near it.'

'S'pose,' Linda kicked as a stone in the path. 'Shame though. If'n we could get the water out it'd make a smashing camp.'

'Too far,' said Len. We'd have t'walk a mile every time we wanted t' go there. Nah. We've got better places'n that closer to 'ome. Warn't us Fran … Francis?'

We halted, suddenly aware that one of our number was lagging some way behind. He was standing in the lane bundling something in his coat oblivious to the rain soaking his shirt.

'What a got?' Linda hurried back, with Len and I close behind. She got close and peered at the bundle in his arms, a smile spreading across her face. 'Tis ol' Mus Reynolds He's only a bitty one, an' all.' She looked around her. 'Out on his own?'

'In broad daylight,' Francis added. 'He looks poorly. I expect he's lost his mother and come out to find food.'

'Watcha gonna do with it?' Len asked.

'Take him home, of course.'

'Don't let no one see you, bwoy. You won't be in good sights if any of en round 'ere knows you've got Reynolds in your 'ouse.'

'Don't care,' Francis hugged the cub to his chest, smoothing its fur with slow strokes of his long, slender fingers. 'It was lying there in the grass, and it's so skinny. I'm not going to leave it to die' He begun stroking the cub's trembling head with circular strokes of his thumb; ignoring the rattle of high-pitched growls that light contact evoked. 'I've always wanted a fox cub for a pet. I never had the chance before.'

'Won't your dad act up?' Linda said.

'No. He doesn't agree with hunting, except perhaps drag-hunting.'

Linda sniffed dismissively. 'Thought ee were a soldier?'

'He was. Doesn't mean he likes killing things. He says he had enough of that.'

'My old dad says only weirdo's go up at drag-'untin'.'

'So do a lot of other people,' Francis replied. 'So what?' He turned away, shielding the cub from her. 'I'm off home. See you.' He struck off across the fields toward his house without another word.

'Oooooh! Antsy-pants,' said Linda.

I frowned at her. 'Well, I think he's roight,' I said. 'You can't kill a liddle biddy fox cub just cos some folks don't like en.'

'Yeah? You wait till ee's in your dad's hen coop. You won't be so 'appy then.'

'Won't so.'

'Will too. So there. You're talkin' rubbish. I'm going 'ome.' She flounced across the lane to the footpath leading toward her own house.

'You'll get wet,' I called after her.

'Already am,' she shouted back, and was gone, over the style and hidden by the high hedge.

'Stroppy lot s'afternoon,' Len observed. 'Come on. We'd better get 'ome an' all or Mum'll go mad. You know 'ow she gets. She'll be spitting when she see how wet you've got.'

He trudged off down the lane and I followed, reluctantly. I hated the fact that my frequent illness made me the target for so many dos and don'ts. Don't go out without a vest and don't forget your coat; where's your hat and so on. 'Oh well' I said to Len. 'Maybe Mum'll be out when we got back, and I c'n dry my clothes off first.

I refused to let maybe spoil the afternoon. It had been worth a nag or two, what with grenades and fox cubs and all kinds of things that the day had never promised when we had started out.

Oak Leaf or Walnut Leaf Wine

2 gall of oak or walnut leaves that are just turning colour

4 lb of Demerara sugar

1 oz of root ginger

1 oz of yeast

1 gall of boiling water

Method

1. Put the leaves in a crock

2. Pour over the boiling water

3. Stand for two or three days in a warm dry place

4. Strain, add the ginger and sugar and boil for 30 minutes

5. When lukewarm add the yeast and leave for one week

6. Strain the liquid into a fermentation jar with a lock

7. When fermentation has finished bottle and store for one year

8. Note: I have tried oak leaf wine and it is a light, dry wine. But given walnut's reputation, and the uses it has been put to in the past I have not been very keen on trying that one, though my aunt insisted she has and lived to tell the tale.

Medicinal – Walnut

Records show that walnuts, in various guises, were used to cure: eczema, hair loss, intestinal worms, quinsy, plague, sore throats, ear infections, fits, ulcers, colic, rabies and wind. Powerful stuff – I will leave it to you to make up your own mind.

Herbalists recommend that the leaves are used in an infusion for eye inflammations and to promote appetite, as a wash for eczema, grazes and bruises.

Outer nut rind (infusion) for diarrhoea or as an anaemia tonic.

Used as a hair rinse to prevent hair loss.

Nut (oil) for menstrual dysfunction or dry eczema.

Inner bark (decoction or tincture) for constipation, liver stimulant and skin diseases.

Medicinal – Oak

Oak is thought to be a good cure for stomach upsets, to break up kidney stones, to reduce inflammations and to stop bleeding.

Grated acorns in warm milk was thought to cure diarrhoea.

Boil six leaves in water and drink it cured ringworm.

The water remaining after boiled bark and leaves of oak was used to cure sores on horses, especially on shoulders.

Traditional – Walnut

According to historical records walnut leaf infusion was once used in Sussex variously as weed killer, insecticide and as a human dwarfing agent (dwarfed children were sold to freak shows).

It was also considered dangerous, by old folks in Sussex to sleep under a walnut tree as it would steal your brains as you slept.

Given the toxic qualities of walnuts this may not have been as silly as it sounds, though I cannot find any record of death by walnuts (barring the kind of allergic shock that can occur with any foods). Better safe than sorry however. If in doubt – don't.

A falling walnut tree was said to herald disaster.

Walnut was also used as a dye and was popular because it did not require a mordant.

Traditional – Oak

Most oak tree legends are either to do with weather or escaping persons. Weather, as in:

Oak before ash – is only a splash
Ash before oak – we're sure for a soak

Or: if the oak leaves drop late it's because the old man oak is holding onto an extra blanket against a promised winter or bad snows.

Oak is regarded in many folk legends a protector, as in the oak that hid Charles II when he fled Cromwell's army.

Oak Apple Day, 29th of May, commemorates his return in 1660.

Sherwood also has the ancient oak purported to be the hide-out of Robin Hood and his band.

Scallops & Raspberry Pie

'There's three big pies in here.'

My mother handed over a wicker basket, its contents covered with a snow-white cloth and tapped the handle, as she added, 'Two raspberry and one cherry. Mind you don't drop them.'

'No Mum.' I took it from her very carefully, lodged it into the carrier on the front of my bike, making sure all was secure, before stepping astride the bicycle.

My mother turned to Len pressed a ten-shilling note firmly into his palm. 'I want three bags of preserving sugar. Got that? It must be preserving sugar. And I want all the change back, mind.'

Len sighed and nodded. 'Okay,' he said. 'Is that all?'

'Yes. See our Susan to the stop and then straight down the village and back. I want to get this last lot of jam made before your Dad gets in for dinner.'

'Can I buy a comic? Fer goin'?'

'Comics? I buy you *Eagle* every week. What else do you want?'

'Well ... *Topper*'s got a model plane kit this week.'

'Bit of old balsa wood, I'll be bound.'

'Yeah, but she's goin' on a trip out. Bain't fair.'

'Oh ... all right. Get your comic. But that's all. No sweets.'

I let out a dramatic sigh. 'Come on, Len. I'm going to miss the coach.'

'Not if it's anything like you,' Len replied. He launched away from the gate and pedalled furiously. 'Slow coach,' he yelled back at me.

'Bye Mum.' I hesitated, wondering if I should hug her, like they did on the TV programmes. Mum was already backing into the kitchen her hand raised in a brief farewell. I shrugged. My mother was like no TV mum I'd ever seen. In fact my entire family was unlike any TV family, with the possible exception of the Beverley Hills's Clampetts. Len was already breaching the first rise, and vanishing out of sight.

'Wait.' I pushed off after him, wobbling with the unaccustomed weight of the wicker basket over my front wheel. 'Wait, Len. Not so fast. It's not fair. I've got stuff to carry.'

I wove a careful path through the ruts and flints that made up the surface of the lane, trying hard not to shake up the precious pies, not fall off my bike and catch up with Len at the same time. It didn't matter to me if Len went on ahead when I knew the way to the bus stop as well as he did.

I was glad he wasn't coming with us to Littlehampton. He never went to Sunday school, whereas I went every week. I wasn't sure why I had to go when my brother didn't, but today it all seemed to be worthwhile. I had earned my place on the annual outing by collecting a full compliment of gummed paper pictures in my attendance book. Those with more than five gaps in their books only got places if there were empty seats. Those that didn't go to Sunday school had no chance at all.

I smiled, feeling a vivid pride in my attendance record with the only gaps appearing when I'd been ill. I felt better suddenly, and freewheeled down the hill without any worry about catching my brother. Len was waiting at the end of the lane, sitting astride his bike, scowling at me. 'You could hurry a little bit,' he said.

'Don't need to wait for me now,' I replied. 'I know the way.'

'Yeah. And Mum'd kill me if you got knocked down,' he replied. 'Now get a wiggle on.'

'Good thing if she did, bossy-boots.' I stood on the pedals and moved a little faster. Not far to go and there was a big downhill stretch to the pub. That was where I would leave my bike and wait for the coach.

The Church always used the ancient pre-war coach

belonging to the Grammar School. Nobody liked the 'Grammar' bus with its slatted wood seats and next to no suspension, and smelling so strongly of diesel inside as well as out; which has to be biggest cause of travel sickness known to man.

Mode of travel aside I was excited. I was luckier than most having Aunt Joan living by the sea, whom we visited several times a year. For many of my friends this outing was their one, annual, seaside visit.

As we coasted down the hill I could see three figures already at the bus stop; Linda, her mother and also her cousin, Bob Joyce.

I groaned as I realised the implications. Bob was a year younger than we were but tall for his age, almost as tall as his aunt, and often thought to be older.

Bob was what the grown-ups referred to as 'a bit slow' and as he stood next to Linda, slack jawed, habitual green snot-candle dribbling from one nostril across his upper lip, it was easy to see why. He clutched an achingly new duffle bag to his chest with both arms and smile big enough to swallow melons. I just knew that Linda and I would be expected to look after him. It was not that I minded, and on another day I might have felt sorry for him, but this was a special trip that I had looked forward to for months. I, somewhat uncharitably, did not want to be lumbered with Bob all day long. *And besides,* I thought, *he hasn't earned his attendance stamps.* I wondered why he wasn't staying with Goody Hurst as he and his brother Eddy often did.

Bob's face woke into a smile as he recognised the cyclists slowing to a halt in front of him.

'Mornin', Mrs Hurst,' Len and I chanted.

'Fish paste,' Bob said proudly before Mrs Hurst could reply.

'What?' I glanced at him, puzzled and hard trying not to sound irritated.

'In my sarnies. Fish paste and *chewcumber*. Auntie Ginny

made en special.'

Len leaned closed and whispered, 'Tough luck. You'm got the dunch in tow.' Out loud he called, 'See yer later,' and cycled toward the village without a backward glance.

I nodded at Bob and shot Linda a commiserating glance before pushing my bike round to the racks at the side of the pub. 'Hello Mrs Hurst,' I said again as I returned. 'You'm coming with us?'

'I am.' She beamed at us. 'So best behaviour, hey, girls?'

We nodded. Mrs Hurst was fun. She liked to join in stuff. 'Why's your Bob yer?' I asked. 'He bain't in our church, nor our school, neither.'

'No he isn't,' Mrs Hurst agreed. 'Bob's mum isn't well. So he's come to stay with us for a while. Vicar said I could bring him today. Give him a little treat.' She patted Bob on the shoulder.

It was generally known that Bob's mum was frequently in hospital, though I had no idea at that age what she was *sick* with, nor which hospital. Only that her stays in hospital were seldom brief affairs. More often she was away for months at a time. I smiled at Bob and he grinned back, waving his bag once again.

'Auntie's made me cake,' he said. 'Sponge.'

'Really?' I glanced at Linda. Your mam made cake?

Linda shook her head. 'Our Jackie made it,' she said. 'Makes a good'n as well. Goody Hurst taught her.'

That was more like it. Jackie under the direction of Mr Hurst's age-crippled dame was more the maternal influence in the Hurst household than Linda's mother.

'They got rolly-costs,' Bob said, peering too-close into my face. 'I sawed it last year. Big, big, way up there, it were.' He flailed his arms around, almost dropping his precious bag. 'I'm going to the rolly-cost.'

I looked to Mrs Hurst. 'Rolly-cost?' I asked.

'Fun fair.'

'Ah.' I patted Bob on the head. 'S'right, Bob.' I patted him again and turned firmly away. The only way to shut Bob up when he started on a subject was to avoid eye contact. 'What else d'you bring?' I asked Linda.

'Pop,' Linda said. 'Lots of fizzy-pop.'

'Lemon pop?' I asked.

'Arr,' said Linda. 'And Dandelion and Burdock, and some Ginger.'

'Cor. I got pies. Raspberry an' cherry.' I lifted the basket to Linda's nose. 'Mum made en.'

'Smashin' and…' The rest of Linda's comment was lost as the coach hissed to a halt beside us

'Hello, hello, hello.' Mr Bailey, Haltwood's long and lean vicar, bounced down the steps to greet us, flapping his arms with more than usual exuberance. 'Luggage in the back.' He galloped off to the boot of the coach and lifted the door. Inside was already heaped with a raft of bags and boxes and baskets. Linda and I loaded the pop and cakes and pies and ran around to the front to scramble into the coach, lest it went without us. Mrs Hurst and Bob had seats reserved at the front with the adults. Linda and I had to search for our own.

The coach was not full, which didn't surprise us. In late July, with the harvest just beginning, older kids were all out helping in fields, and the youngest could not come without their mothers, so it was all down to the seven to elevens who were free to go 'gadding', as Linda's dad had put it. It did mean we had our pick near to the rear of the bus.

We were not sorry to be thin on the ground. It meant a day without the burden of elder sibling menace and we settled eagerly and joined in with the singing that had temporarily paused long enough for us to be picked up.

Mr Bailey mostly had us rattling out old standards like, *This little light of mine* or *If you're happy and you know it*. It didn't matter that it was hymns when it wasn't a Sunday. They felt less like hymns than battle cries as we rattled along the road towards the sea.

*

The tide was on the ebb when we finally arrived so that once the food and bags had been piled onto the pebbly upper beach we had a vast expanse of shingle and sand to cross before we could touch a single toe into the brine. Before that, however, we were required to endure the Reverend Bailey's 'little chat'.

'A few words,' He beamed at us, hands clasped behind his back. 'We shall, of course, be having games on the beach. Little bit of cricket, that sort of thing. And I know some of you little ones are raring to get started on your sandcastle competition. But before you all rush away, a few notices. We shall have lunch at one, so if you would all stay in sight of this spot that would be absolutely smashing.' He pointed at his feet. 'Don't want to lose anyone, do we?'

'Don't ee go on,' Linda whispered.

'Same speech as last year,' I held up a finger. 'Hold on. Here comes the river, fair, and traffic bit.

'Now, children, a few simple rules. Please stay away from the river. The Arun is a very dangerous piece of water as you well know, but doubly so here. Also, please don't be tempted to head for the fair on your own. We shall all be paying a short visit there before we leave; but all together please. No prizes for guessing what I have to say about the sea.' He looked around expectantly. 'Anyone?'

'No paddling without an adult,' a voice called.

'Exactly. Do not enter the water unless there is an adult on hand. And last of all please do not go back to the bus on your own. The coach park is very dangerous. Now,' he clapped his hands, 'lunch in one hour, so off you go. Mrs Fletcher will blow her whistle when we want you all back here to eat. Any questions?'

'Can I go to the rolly-cost?'

Mr Bailey looked down at Bob, smiling tightly. 'Rolly what, Robert?'

'Roller coaster,' Mrs Hurst said. 'He's been on about

nothing else all the way here.'

'No, not now, Robert. We shall go to the fair later on. I have explained that.'

'I wanna go now. I got a sixpence.' Bob stood square before the vicar, one grubby hand extended to display his riches. With the other hand he wiped at the candle, which was, so far as anyone could tell, a permanent fixture even in the height of summer.

'Oh. Right. Roller-coaster, of course.' He patted Bob's head, hesitantly. His throat bobbing as he swallowed hard. 'Later, Robert, I promise you will have your ride. Now, any *other* questions?'

'No, Mr Bailey.' A slow ragged chorus echoed out the expected reply, and within seconds two dozen children had scattered across the sand before he could think of any additions to his list of restrictions.

All except for Bob that was, who stood staring at Mr Bailey for several seconds before he trotted off after his cousin.

Linda glanced behind her and sighed. 'Bugger,' she muttered. 'I thought we might've lost en.'

'Not that lucky,' I said.

Bob scurried to overtake us and walked backwards so that he could face us as he talked. 'Can we go to the rolly-cost now?'

'Mr Bailey already said no, Bob. You just wait,' Linda snapped. 'Now stop goin' on about that they rolly-cost, will you?'

'But it en't very far.' Bob pointed up the beach and past the coach park toward the fairground, where the metal skeleton of his precious rolly-cost rose clearly above the mass. Next to it, just a fraction shorter, stood the red and white 'lighthouse' striped helter-skelter. The fairground was tempting us all too varying degrees. I could just make out two brightly coloured cars crawling up one of the roller-coaster tracks trundling along the top before turning at the end of the straight and dropping sharply. I heard the screams of the occupants as they plummeted earthwards ... though that may have been the mews soaring overhead.

I looked firmly away toward the waves, and watched a gaggle of white and black birds swooping on the wind, reminding me of rooks playing above the woods near Kiln Field, except these birds did not soar in the warm air above a harvest field.

The breeze coming off the sea was cool and sharp. I breathed in and wrinkled my nose at the seaweed stench. We were still very close to the high tideline, where swathes of bladder wrack and kelp were washed up in black, salt encrusted, heaps. We would need to move further down the sand to avoid the plagues of flies and sand hoppers that infested these sea-sculpted middens.

I had moved on to fresh interests. Bob was still extolling the virtues of the fair. 'It's a big, big, rolly-cost...'

I grabbed him by the shoulder and brought my face close to his. 'Bob,' I said quietly. 'I tell you what. Go and tell your Auntie Ginny she wants you.'

'Okay.' Bob smiled and trotted obediently up the beach toward the adults, who were busy setting out the striped deckchairs and windscreens near to the breakwater.

'Run,' Linda hissed.

And we ran, striking out diagonally across the beach to the next breakwater. At its lowest point, close to where the tide was washing the sand we jumped up and over the cracked and pitted black timbers, and crouched on the far side, giggling and breathless.

'Think we lost en?' Linda was peering back over toward the beach we had just crossed.

'I reck'n,' said I. 'Can you see him?'

'He's just reached mum,' Linda began giggling again. 'He fell fer it.'

'He always does,' I replied. 'Shame really.'

'No 'tain't. He can help the babes make sandcastles. He'll

like that.'

'Of course.'

We fell silent, guilty for a few seconds but not in any way truly repentant. The water was too inviting. We ripped off sandals and socks and leapt to our feet, and placing discarded footwear carefully on top of the breakwater we edged into the sandy-brown of the English Channel. We tucked skirts into knicker-legs and waded out into the water, knee deep, shrieking as the waves swelled the water up to our thighs, wetting skirts and knickers alike.

The water was cold, despite it being a hot July day, and very soon our knees and feet had turned a bright salmon pink. We splashed out onto the sand, shivering and laughing.

'Oh look.' Linda darted forward and held up a tiny pair of still-hinged scallop shells, creamy-pink and delicately frilled. I untucked my skirt and held it before me with one hand, dropping my finds into the hollow made by the wet cloth.

'And a razor.' I added a thin blue razor shell to the collection.

We retrieved our footwear and paced along the sand searching the shore, stopping every few feet to pick up or discard new finds. Shells, crab legs, coloured stones. All were eagerly scooped up and examined. We had gone quite a distance when the faint shrill of the lunch whistle cut through the constant wash of the waves. By that time both of us had gathered a mass of sand-encrusted treasures. We were more than happy to scuttle back to the picnic spot and tip the horde into a tin seaside bucket painted in garish blue and yellow that Linda had left with her bag.

There seemed to be enough laid out there to feed several coach loads. Sandwiches and pies and cakes of all descriptions covered two large trestle tables, covered in snow white cloths, which were pinned to the table legs with ruthless efficiency. The table legs were in turn rammed firmly into the pebbles of the beach and weighted with large rocks. They were going nowhere despite the stiff breeze. Surveying the food with wide eyes we suddenly realised how hungry we were.

'That's quite a haul of shells, girls,' Mrs Fletcher called. 'You've been busy. Now you can keep busy if you like and help with the plates.'

'Yes, Miss.' We surged forward to take a bundle of paper plates to hand out to the ragged line of children that had formed by instinct at one end of the food. The Haltwood Sunday School outing made short work of lunch. Soon we were lazing in the sun while the adults brewed tea on hissing primus stoves.

'Tis black over Will's aunt's,' Linda observed.

I was staring up at the sky, and a line of dark-grey scuds gathering over the sea. I turned my head away from the small yachts I had been watching cruising at the river mouth, waiting for the turning tide to allow them back up to their moorings. 'Is it going to rain, then?'

Linda shook her head. 'Not yet.'

I was satisfied. Linda had an uncanny knack with weather prediction that her grandmother had taught her. That was not all people thought Goody Hurst knew, but I didn't believe all the gossip. I'd never seen any evidence of Goody owning a besom, much less flying it. I watched the infants busily adding the finishing touches to sand castles. 'Wan'na make one?' I asked, without much conviction. Both Linda and I considered ourselves too dignified for castle building with the infants. Though watching industrious tots excavate and decorate with such sublime dedication I had to admit, if only to myself, that it looked very tempting.

Linda shook her head again. 'I want to have another scout for scallops, fer my Dad as an ash tray. The tide'll be on the turn soon, so we have to look now.'

I levered myself to my feet, dusting sand from tanned, bare legs. In all the times I had walked the beaches of the Sussex coast the only larger shells I'd ever found were the well-polished blue and pink remains of oysters and even they would barely cover my palm. I was sure Linda would be disappointed, but there was always a first time. 'Okay. Shall we go along the high tide line or down further?'

'Anywhere, but let's be quick.' She jerked her head toward Bob, sitting in the midst of the sandcastle 'city' constructing an imposing edifice of his own. 'When they've judged them they castles, we'll 'ave 'im unless we get off now.' Linda grabbed a spare tin bucket. 'Ready?'

There was not a lot of point in arguing with Linda when she had on her bossy hat. I sighed but followed. I could not help feeling guilty in dodging out of the special responsibility we'd been given but, I supposed, it wasn't like there were not plenty of grown-ups around to keep an eye. And besides, we might get dragged into one of the Reverend's interminable cricket tournaments.

I always disliked team games. Not because I didn't like the teams as such, or playing games, because I did on the whole. I avoided team sports for the far deeper reason that I could not abide the bickering. It didn't much matter which game was being played, the grousing was always along the same lines: 'She was out'; 'He's cheating'; 'He wasn't in the crease'; 'the ball bounced', and so on and so forth. Why they couldn't just get on with it I could never understand. So much playing time was wasted in griping and sniping.

Linda was vanishing along the lee side of the breakwater and I hurried to catch her up. I could hear the Reverend calling a gathering to pick teams. We had barely escaped in time. Ducking slightly to keep below the wooden palisades, we were two breakwaters distant from the main group before we deemed themselves far away enough to be safe.

We searched for almost an hour, scouring the beach for that elusive scallop. Forced higher up the pebbles by the encroaching tide we were close to the promenade when Linda finally admitted defeat.

'Only biddy bits,' Linda said, shaking her bucket full of half-shells and pearly slivers. 'I don't know what we can get. I promised 'im a shell.' She gazed up the beach, past the painted beach-huts, toward the promenade 'Got any money?' She pointed toward the very top of the slope at a collection of single-story white-painted shops.

'Not much,' I said. 'Enough for a few rides.'

'Well have a few less. Come one.'

The shops were selling all of the usual beach fare. A sweet stall selling pink sticks of rock, a tea stall, a chippy and several emporia offering buckets and spades and other paraphernalia deemed essential for a day on the beach. But the shop that had attracted Linda's attention was smaller than the rest and set slightly aside. It was a little more run down, its stucco walls flaking, its door that may once have been blue, had devolved to a washed out grey that was cracked and peeling.

On the beach-ward side the single word SHELLS was displayed large black letters. Linda pushed through the door, and after only a small hesitation I followed.

The interior was gloomy after the harsh sunlight of the outer world, and made all the dimmer by the deep browns and blacks of the lovingly polished display cases. Rows of shells of all sizes and types, many of designs that neither of us had ever seen before, curling horns and hinged cases and shimmering bivalves, all nestled in tissue paper nests beneath the glass counter top or one of the many enclosed shelves that lined the walls.

Near to the door stood a row of wicker baskets heaped high with less exotic wares. Linda dived forward to extract a scallop from a wicker bin. She held it up, glancing at me excitedly. 'Tis all shiny inside,' she breathed. 'Look'.

Linda traced the rippling lines on the barnacle-pitted surface with her thumb nail. The dull grey outside was somewhere between oatmeal and concrete in both texture and colour. Turning it over revealed an interior that was smooth and opalescent, its colours blending from rich cream at the narrowest edge through pink and mauve to a gleaming yellow-brown at the crinkled outer edge. Linda picked one of the slate grey remnants from her bucket and held it next to the complete shell for comparison.

'Don't look like the same beast,' I observed.

'Yet it is.'

Linda jumped at the unrecognised voice, almost dropping the shell. I grabbed at her arm and we both took an involuntary step toward the door.

The Shell Man was one of those people who could have been any age between twenty-five and forty, which by Linda and my standards made him pretty old. He wore a faded blue shirt and pale cream trousers and sandals of a kind we had never seen before, flat roped soles with a plaited string thong looped over his biggest toe. His face and arms were the colour of pale toffee that made the fine down of fair hair along his forearms glitter like gold thread. He was not tall, but slim and muscular, with sandy hair curling around his ears in a decidedly bohemian fashion. He was like nothing either of us had seen before.

'Of the genus Pecten.' The vision added. He came out from behind the counter and gently took the shell from Linda's limp hands. 'You don't see them whole on the beach too often around here, even after storms. Not the big ones like this anyway.' He returned the shell and smiled at us.

I felt my insides shiver. And I knew I was staring. I was also aware that my mouth was hanging open. I shut it abruptly, and felt my cheeks reddening. I had never come across anyone who had made me feel so awkward. He spoke to us as an equal, and that was something quite new.

Linda was far less in awe. 'You don't pick them up round here then?'

'No, we get these from the fishermen. The scallop boats dredge up lots of shells along with the live ones.'

'What do them catch en for?' Linda demanded.

'To eat, or rather to sell to other people to eat.' He smiled, tilting his head to look at us in amused silence for a moment. 'Some people think they are quite a delicacy. The restaurants pay good money for them.'

'Like whelks?'

He laughed sharply. 'Sort of but a lot more expensive. They say…' He paused. 'Well, never mind what they say.' He leaned back on the counter. 'You wanted to buy one?'

Linda shrugged and sniffed, in a passable imitation of her gran's shopping persona. 'Maybe, and maybe not. How much are those big whelks, then?' She pointed at a huge shell in the centre of the rear display.

The man's face twitched. I wondered if he were trying to disguise annoyance or laughter; it was hard to tell. I hung back, just in case it turned out to be the former, wishing to disassociate myself from any potential blunders. The object Linda had pointed out was, I had to admit, very like a huge spotted version of a common whelk at first glance, but with longer and more decorative horns protruding from around the spiral. It gleamed, brown and mauve, nestling in its snow-white paper nest. I had the feeling it was something way beyond ordinary.

'That is a conch shell.' He picked a smaller, and less vivid, version from the counter top and held it out to Linda. 'Hold it to your ear.'

She looked at him doubtfully as she took it. 'Why?'

'To hear the sea,' he replied.

Linda glanced at me, hesitant, ready to be scathing if occasion demanded.

I nodded. I had read all about seashells and how you would hear the ocean if you held the coiled opening to you ear. I had also read how, when blown through, conch shells had summoned many a sea god, or monster in books that I had borrowed from the meagre school library. 'Robinson Crusoe had one,' I said.

'Quite right,' the Shell Man, jerked his head in a curt nod of approval. 'And did you know that in some places shells are, or rather were, used instead of money?'

I giggled. 'Go on.'

'Really they do.' He ran his fingers through a small pot of shells in a dish near the till. 'Cowrie shells,' he said. 'Cypraea moneta. Just think. No asking for pocket money. You could just run down to the beach and find your own.' He smiled at me and winked.

I smiled back. It was the sort of joke that my father tried all the time. 'Not any more?' I said. 'They use money now?'

'Sadly, yes. Or I could be very rich.'

'You've got a shop though.'

The Shell Man laughed. 'My father has the shop. I am but a humble scientist.' He bowed, a mocking bow of cavalier standards, doffing a make-believe plumed hat almost to the floor. Both of us began to giggle.

'What sort of science?' I asked. 'Rockets and stuff?'

'Nothing so grand. I study oceans. Or at least the things that live in them.'

'Oh.' I thought about that for a moment. It was not a job I had ever thought existed. 'So you're still a sort of a shell man?'

Again that twitch of eye and lip. 'A shell man?' he mused. 'A man of shell?' He nodded. 'I guess I am, in an odd sort of way.'

'Cor.' I gazed at him, not sure what else I could say. 'Do they have shell ladies as well?'

'Lots.' He scooped a handful of shells from the bowl and dropped them into my hand. 'Here. A present. Work hard at school, and get lots of exams. And then...' The shop bell jangled loudly as door opened in a big hurry.

'There you are. We've been looking all over for you.' Mrs Hurst was hot and breathless. 'We said not to come up on the road.'

'But Mum.' Linda slid on her most wheedling tone as easily as dragging on a well-worn shoe. 'I promised Dad a shell fer 'is fags ... and there weren't none on the beach. We was comin' straight back. Honest. We weresn't lost. Not no how.'

'Were not,' Mrs Hurst replied, absently. 'Never mind that. Have you got Bob with you?'

'No. He was making castles with the liddle babs.'

'Well he isn't now.' She rubbed steepled fingers against her brows and sighed. 'Who knows where he's gone.'

'A child missing?' the Shell Man asked.

Mrs Hurst started, as if she had only just noted his existence. 'Yes. We are on a Sunday school trip, and there is always a few that bend the rules. Like these two.' She paused to glare at us. 'But this is different. Robert is a young lad-- with problems. He's not like this pair of ruthless pirates.' She frowned at us again, but with an odd quirk to her mouth that reminded me of the Shell Man's ambiguous expressions. 'These two are like bad pennies. They will always show up again. But poor young Robert.' She spread her hands wide.

'He's not all there,' Linda said, tapping the side of her head. 'Got a few marbles missin'.'

Mrs Hurst grabbed her daughter's arm and shook it, making the shell drop to the bare wood floor with a high clink. 'Linda Hurst, how many times must I tell you? Do not say things like that.'

'Tis true, though, Mum,' she replied. 'Ee bain't all there.' She took a pace back, half expecting a slap.

Mrs Hurst only shook her head.

'From the mouths of babes?' The Shell Man asked.

She nodded. 'I had better get these two back, so the vicar knows we only have one escapee and not three. Why it's always my tribe that gets into these things I do not know. It's like herding quicksilver on a hillside.'

'You just can't stop some minds wandering,' he replied. 'And the bodies invariably follow. Can I help at all?'

'Very kind, but no. We should get back first and see what's happening.'

'Then be quick. If you need to call the coast guard you should do it before the tide turns. It goes at one hell of a speed along this stretch so near the river.'

'I hope we won't need to. But thanks.' Mrs Hurst opened the door. 'Girl's?'

'But Dad's shell.' Linda said, 'I promised 'im.'

The Shell Man retrieved the fallen scallop and presented it to her.

'A present for you as well. Just promise to do all your homework. Can you promise me that? Both of you?'

'Promise.'

*

We knew we were in trouble. Mrs Hurst marched us down the prom in stony silence, so fast we were almost running.

I shoved the cowries into my pocket and held them through the cloth, terrified they might jump out and be lost. All the while my mind centred on the Shell Man and his shop. He was a strange man, almost magical. He reminded me a little of the man on the TV who did animal programmes (though his name eluded me). What was important was that he had been someone who talked to us. He had told us stuff without any need for complicated questioning, imparting knowledge as freely as shells to both me and to Linda.

I trotted after Mrs Hurst and Linda, the comforting shapes of a half dozen cowries in my pocket crystallising my promises to myself. I would be someone. Do something. Provided we lived to see the day out. Arriving at the beach I took in a scene of complete turmoil.

'Oh, Virginia. You found the girls.' Reverend Bailey bounded across the beach to meet us, arms flapping wildly. 'No sign of poor young Robert?'

Mrs Hurst shoved us toward the main group, a gesture of disdain that hurt me deeply. I knew we should, perhaps, not have been in that shop, but we had hardly committed a crime – and we were not responsible for Bob if he had wandered off.

Mrs Hurst moved further down the beach. 'No, the girls insist they have not seen him since lunch.' She shot us one final grimace, daring us to move from the spot, and went down to the edge of the water with the Reverend.

'They all think en's drowned,' said Angela Cartwright. 'Wandered off lookin' for you two an' fell in the water. You ain't half going to get it when your ol' dad gets you, Linda Hurst. Ee'll be that mad.'

'Taint my fault,' Linda snapped. 'I didn't push en.'

I inserted myself between Linda and the 'arch-bitch Angela'. There was a bubbling in Linda's voice that spoke of tears, and I was not having that. 'Leave her be. Tisn't her fault.'

'Ee was off lookin' fer you. So there, tis so.'

'Tisn't.' I let Linda go and advanced toward the taller girl.

Angela backed off. I was small, but my temper was legendary, but she could not go without a parting shot. 'We'll see. Toffee-nose. When they've fished him out – dead.'

'No,' Linda grabbed at my skirt. 'Leave 'er be. Tis part our fault, Susie. We did run off'n leave, when me mam asked us to look out fer en.'

I shook my head. I was not going to have that. It wasn't our fault. Not any how. Him and his bloody stupid rolly-cost. Of course. He'd talked about nothing else. How could no one have thought of it? Grown-ups could be dense sometimes, always looking on the black side of every thing. I grabbed Linda by both hands. 'That's where he is. At the rolly-cost.'

'What?'

'Your Bob. I bet he's gone off after that fun fair. Mrs Hurst, Mrs Hurst. We know where he is!'

*

'I should have thought. It never even entered my head.' Mrs Hurst strode through the crowd at a nerve-wracking speed, with Linda and me trailing in her wake, terrified that we too would be lost in the crush. Linda had talked us both into the rescue mission on the grounds that Bob, should he imagine he might be in trouble, would not come back to an adult. He had run wild to avoid a telling off many times, a habit born of a father who had been less than lenient with the strap before he had deserted wife and sons. It was no secret that the abandonment had also been the start of Bob's mother's unmentionable illness that resulted in her long absences in hospital.

That was then, this was now, and hardly time to think of anything but keeping up with Mrs Hurst's rapid progress. We barely had time to notice the fair, with its stalls and rides at every turn. Not that we would have got truly lost because, as Linda pointed out a little breathlessly. 'We c'n hardly miss the thing, can we?'

That was true enough. Towering above us, it was far larger than either of us remembered from last year, which was odd, because things usually seemed to get smaller in my experience; such as the wall in front of Gran's house that had been huge when I was four, and now hardly came above my waist. We stopped near the queue waiting for rides and looked around.

'Can't see him,' Mrs Hurst muttered. 'Where is that damned boy?'

'Up there,' Linda replied, pointing to the cars on the tracks above us. We could just make out Bob's pale face before the car jerked around the next bend and was out of sight.

'Thank God.' Mrs Hurst sagged visibly as the fear left her. 'Linda? Can you find your way back to the Reverend and tell him we've seen Robert, and we will be back with him shortly?'

'Yes, Mam.' Linda smiled at me before ducking away.

I watched her go, a little envious, knowing my mother would never trust me that way. We waited, Mrs Hurst's gaze fixed on the roller coaster ride, as if afraid that Bob would jump free and vanish before I could grab him. My attention was more taken by the sights, sounds and smells all around us.

The loud, brash, music of the rides accompanied by a roar

of so many voices raised to compete for space in the seething mass. The shouts of stall keepers mingled with the shrieks of holiday makers on rides; the sharp crack of airguns from a shooting stall nearby; bells pinging from the open doors of a penny arcade across the way. And yes, those smells. Cloying sweetness of rock and floss at the candy stall just a few feet away vied with the acrid tang of machine oil and the rank stench of shellfish, whelks and winkles and jellied eels.

I wrinkled my nose at the latter. I have never liked the fish odour. I wondered in passing if the Shell Man liked the smell of fish. Maybe he had to, if he spent so much time in or by the sea. I felt a smile cross my lips as I thought about him. My attention was jerked back to reality as the roller coaster carriages slowed to a halt.

Mrs Hurst waited for Bob to come through the barrier, and as he started back toward the queue for another ride before she pounced. 'Robert. We have been worried sick. You should not go off without telling us.'

Robert stood motionless for a moment, stunned. Trapped. I knew the feeling of being caught in the act. I, in that situation, would be sifting alibis at top speed for a plausible excuse.

I took his other arm and we began to pull him to one side. Bob's reaction stunned me, as it did almost everyone around us.

'Don't 'it me. Please Auntie, don't 'it me, I'll be good, Honest. I didn't mean to do nuthin'. I just wanted to see the rolly-cost.'

He was blubbering, crouched against the ride's white wood fence, both his arms drawn over his head and shoulders, cringing away from his aunt in, so far as I could tell, genuine terror.

'Don't 'it me. Please don't 'it me.' He was almost incoherent, snot and tears flowing freely in twin streams down his scarlet face.

Mrs Hurst and I glanced around us, aghast. There were murmurings rising within the crowd. Mutterings and dark looks aimed not at the miscreant, Robert, but at Mrs Hurst.

She knelt beside Bob, her hand held out, not quite touching him, seemingly afraid that a physical contact might send him fleeing through the crowd. 'No one will hurt you, Robert. It's all right. No one will hurt you. We were worried, that's all. Calm down, please. No one will hurt you. We promise. Come on now. If you calm down right away we'll go back to the beach. There are some cakes left. Some of Jackie's nice cake. You'd like that wouldn't you?'

Bob cringed further away. As his sobbing grew louder so the audience's mood? Humour became a little uglier.

Mrs Hurst looked around at me, an appeal in her eyes that I did not quite understand. Adults were not supposed to look to kids for help. She kept up her soothing monologue, in the way that my father did with spooked stock. The words probably made as much sense to Robert as they would to a sheep. It was plain he was not listening, but the tone had a similar hypnotic effect on him.

Gradually the screams and sobs quietened into heaving hiccoughs of emotion. The crowd remained, looking on in judgement. The mutterings from that crowd continued. I wanted to shout at them all to shut up. They didn't understand the situation any more than Bob. Mrs Hurst was the nicest person, and she would never hurt anyone. These people had no right to judge her. Just because Bob's old man had knocked him a round a bit, didn't mean the whole family were slap-happy.

I could sympathise. Whilst my father would never dream of chastising me physically, my mother kept a cane in the kitchen drawer, and I had felt its bite on several occasions. Probably not as hard, or as often, as the beatings that Bob seemed to fear, but often enough to understand his feelings in some measure. I became aware that I was closest to understanding him of any one present.

I crouched beside him and rummaged in my pocket for a suitable bribe. 'Bob,' I whispered. 'Bob, it's me, Susie...

Linda's gone to fetch the Reverend. You don't want the Reverend to see yer all upset, d'you? It's our outin' day, Bob. You've bin lookin' forward to this for ages I'll bet. Don't cry. Please don't cry. No one'll 'it you. Specially not your Auntie Ginny. You know that, don't you? She bain't like your ole' dad. She's nice. An' the Reverend's nice, an' so's our Linda ... mostly.' I let myself laugh lightly, drawing Bob a little more upright despite his efforts to remain curled in a foetal ball. 'It's a nice day, Bob. An' you can't spoil it fer us all with all this blubbering. Tell you what. I bet the Reverend's got some pennies for candyfloss. You loikes candy floss doncha Bob? I bet if you was to stop all that noise that old Rev'd buy you some. For bein' so brave'n that. 'Ere, I got a pressie. Look. Shells.' I held one of my precious cowries out to him, just inches from his nose, which was no longer candled so much as torrenting.

The sobs slowed, and one arm lowered enough for Bob to peer at me cautiously. 'I didn't mean nuthin'. I wanted to see the rolly-cost, was all.'

'We knows that, Bob.'

He looked at the shell and tweaked a tiny smile. 'Is that moine?'

'Yes. All yours if'n you stop that noise 'n get up.' I put two fingers beneath his elbow and stood, slowly, encouraging him to rise. 'Come on Bob. We'll go find the Reverend, shall we? Go an' getcha some candy floss?'

He nodded, wiping his face on his bare arm. Mrs Hurst whipped a hanky from her pocket and gave it to him. 'Lets tidy you up a bit, shall we, Robert? Don't want the Reverend to see you with a grubby face, do we?'

Together we coaxed the trembling boy away from the crowd, pausing only for Mrs Hurst to buy him the cloud of promised floss. He very soon had a liberal smearing of pink sugar added to the snotty remnants across his face, but the trauma of the previous minutes had all been laid to rest.

The excursion back to the fair with the rest of the party was a bit tame by comparison. I enjoyed the rides on the carousel and bumper cars, and used my skills gained with an airgun on rabbits to win two prizes on the shooting stall before I was 'encouraged' by the stall holder to leave.

I wandered with Linda through the crowds. We ate ice cream, bought sticks of rock for our families, and admired the lights that came on at four o'clock, even though it was not even beginning to get dark. But it was not the same. The day's high point was long gone. I felt in my pocket for the remaining shells and sighed. My special gift had been cut down from four shells to three. Precious as gemstones to me I was angry with myself for giving one away, especially when Bob had lost it within half an hour. But it had bought Linda and me a reprieve from sentence over our excursion to the Shell Man. I made sure the remaining three were pushed well down in my pocket and set about helping with repacking the coach.

Going home, the adults tried very hard to raise spirits with some singing, but everyone was tired. By the time we stopped at the common I was more than ready to go home.

I plodded round to the back of the pub to collect my bike and wheeled it back in time to see the Hursts shouldering their bags ready to walk home.

'See you tomorrow?' Linda asked.

I nodded, limiting myself to a wave and a brief 'Bye' and then pedalled away. Tomorrow we would begin collecting our Sunday school stamps for the next trip.

Cherry Wine

10 lb of sweet cherries

2 lb of loaf sugar

1 teaspoon of yeast

Method

1. Wash the cherries, stone and chop them into a bowl over a pan of water. Heat them.

2. When the juice starts to run remove the fruit and press it through a cloth, getting as much juice as possible from the pulp (use an apple press if you have one).

3. Strain twice through muslin and make juice up to a gallon with water if necessary.

4. Dissolve sugar into the fruit juice.

5. Cool to lukewarm, put into a crock and add yeast.

6. Cover and leave for three days.

7. Strain into a fermentation vessel with a lock.

8. When fermentation is complete bottle and store for at least six months.

Raspberry Wine

4 lb of raspberries

4 lb of loaf sugar

1 gall of boiling water

Method

1. Pour boiling water over the fruit and mash well and leave for four days, stirring daily.

2. Strain through double muslin into a crock with the sugar.

3. Stir until the sugar is dissolved.

4. Add yeast and cover well. Leave in a warm place for one day.

5. Put into a fermentation vessel with a lock.

6. When fermentation is complete bottle and store for six months.

7. This recipe will work with most soft fruits such as black, red or white currants, blueberries, loganberries etc. Be sure to use clean, un-damaged fruit as these type of berries are prone to moulds other than yeast, and will spoil if they are contaminated.

8. Strawberries require lemon juice and raisins in the first stage.

Medicinal – Cherries

Known cough cure, as well as a sedative and digestive aid. Wild Cherries are said to be more potent than the cultivated varieties.

Medicinal – Raspberries

The leaves have long been associated with easing childbirth. As a tincture it is also used for small wounds, inflammations, ulcers, prostate tonic.

It has laxative and diuretic properties.

Raspberry vinegar is a good cure for sore throats and is a helpful expectorant.

Raspberry leaves should not be used during early pregnancy.

Traditional – Cherries

The Cherry tree was not very lucky; though in more modern times cherry blossom to the Japanese represents the millions killed by atomic blasts that heralded the end of WW2.

To see cherry blossom in autumn portends a severe winter, and it is said that anyone (children in particular) climbing a cherry tree on St James's night would suffer a broken neck.

Children would run around a cherry tree and sing, *Cuckoo cherry tree, Come down and tell me, how many years will I live*. The cuckoo is supposed to supply the answer, or in its absence the tree would be shaken to see how many fruits fell down.

Chanting cherry stones eaten by a girl foretold of her luck in marriage: *This year, next year, sometime, never*.

Raspberries

Raspberries do not seem to have much to do with custom or folklore – their main purpose appears to be tasting good.

A Harvest Supper's Punch

The Sussex-wagon was backed up to the drying stores and huge fifty-six pound hessian sacks of grain were sitting in rabbit-ears rows on the floor of the bar. Sitting on the sacks were a row of equally dusty, ragged harvesters.

Roy Fuller drained his glass of cider and eased himself to his feet. 'Whal. I've got milkin' to do. Can't sit around all day like you bwoys.' He rinsed the glass in a bucket of water set by the door.

'Bain't time yet, Roy. You'm got time fer another 'arf.' Andy Pike sauntered toward the double doors and nodded at my father. 'Ups-a-daisy, Stan?'

My father rose eagerly. 'Don't' mind if I do.' He looked down at me and held a finger to his lips. 'Don't you go sayin' nuthin'. Specially to old Westy.'

I nodded. The taciturn farm foreman was not much liked by the labourers, and I was not keen myself. The Guv'nor would be part of the fun on occasion, such as yesterday when he had helped me in building 'staircases' with straw bales whilst waiting for the trailer to collect the next load. But Bill West or 'Old Westy', would only shout at me to 'get orf' this and 'stop' that. He was a killjoy.

I followed my father into the space between the trailer and the next shed that was known as 'Dirty Dicks' after the infamous London pub. Historically it had been the cider store where the farm-made beverage was made, ready for thirsty throats in the harvest fields. But that year Old Westy had acquired a shiny new Morris Minor, and had persuaded the Guv'nor to allow it to be kept in the Cider shed. And because it was his car, he had not only put a padlock on the shed door, but retained all the keys.

This meant that he could ration the cider to one glass at a time to the farm hands, yet I knew for a fact that Westy regularly collected a quart jug from the store when he thought no one was looking. I also knew that he knew that I knew, and in that conundrum lay the problem. He didn't hold with young girls hiding in haylofts to catch him in his acts of wanton theft, nor with labourers' kids being less stupid than he imagined or wanted them to be. On the other hand, I should not have been where I was at the time. It was a stand off in theory, but it did not help me a great deal. Unpopular didn't begin to describe him for his machinations.

Never daunted Dad, Andy and Roy had devised an easy way to overcome the problem. They grabbed the doors and lifted them from the hinges, swinging both leaves, with the padlocked bar intact, to one side. While Andy and my father held the doors upright, Roy nipped in to refill not only glasses, but three stout, brown, screw-top bottles; each holding a quart of the cloudy, fragrant cider.

Mission accomplished they scuttled back to the drying granary with their ill-gotten gains, chuckling like a flock of excited geese. The second 'unofficial' round was swallowed quickly as the unmistakable throaty chatter of Westy's old Massey Ferguson could be heard in the distance.

'Milkin',' Roy said, and vanished.

'An' we'd better get goin',' said Andy. He swilled out the glasses and set them on the ledge by the door. 'Last load, you reck'n, Stan?'

'One, maybe two,' my father agreed. 'And that'll be None Such and Farm Break done. We'll only have Seven Acre left.'

'What's the bettin' Old Westy wants it done today 'n all,' Andy grumbled. 'We'll be out there till gorn nine and I wuz hopin' to get down to the Supper tonight.' He turned to me and ruffled my hair. 'You workin' down there then, young maid?'

I nodded. 'Don't have to be there till seven. My patrol's not doin' Hall decoratin'. Only table settin'.'

'Lucky then, ain't you?' he laughed. 'Comin' with us now? Your Len's up there already with his mate. We've got the last knockin's on this load.'

I looked to my father, wondering how long he would be. I didn't want to miss anything but my stomach was growling for sustenance.

'Tell you what,' said Dad. 'Come up to None Such on the trailer and then you can get me some sloes. I need another pound or two.'

'Okay.' I grabbed a trug from the shelf and skipped out into the late summer sunshine. I was happy enough to eat rabbit, but was not much keen on 'knocking'; when the lads laid in wait as the combine cut the last triangle of corn at the field's centre. Always, as the last 'knockings' of the harvest fell, the rabbits and pigeons, and even the occasional deer that had taken refuge there, would make a break for safety; into the waiting firing line of the harvesters, men and boys alike, would leap out with rifles or stout sticks and kill as many of them as they were able.

It was easy to see the logic in taking advantage of that largesse, but I found it a harsh part of harvest that I preferred not to indulge in. The fields called None Such and Farm Break, stood on the top of the ridge above our cottage, with Seven Acre lying between those two and Newfarm Lane. I would at least get a lift almost all the way home, which was handy, as I would need to hurry if I were to pick these sloes and still be ready to go out that evening. I hauled myself onto the empty trailer and stood next to my father, mimicking the way he gripped the head rail lightly with one hand with knees slightly bend to absorb the rock and bump of the rough terrain. Stan joined us there, while Andy climbed into the tractor seat.

'See yer later,' Roy called. 'I shall leave out a ticket fer the feeds, Stan.'

'Righto.'

'You milkin' tomorrow morning?' I asked.

'Yes. And then finishing the Seven Acre.'

'You're not comin' to the supper then?'

'Sorry pet. I'd like to, but it's too late when I have to get up at four to milk.'

'What about Len?'

'Helping me, so he said.'

'And Mum won't come.'

He shook his head. 'Doubt it, pet. The Guv'nor's got a house full of guests so she's got extra bedrooms to clean, and breakfast to help with. We'd like to come, but...'

I looked up at him and half smiled. I was disappointed but I was also old enough to realise that that work came first. My father's work on the farm and my mother's in the Big House as housemaid for the Guv'nor's wife was what kept us going. I would still have liked one of the family to be there.

The tractor lurched forward and I automatically flexed my knees a little more to compensate for the swaying of the trailer as we headed out of the main yard toward the rough track that was Newfarm Lane, and trundled into the field just as the combine was finishing a sweep. Clouds of dust rose from around the machine as it swung a wide arc for the final cut. A small stand of corn, triangular in shape waited its final moments. It was wider than the combine's cutter, but only just. Anything left alive among the stalks would need to flee before the scything blades of the Combine.

The tractor and trailer had ground to a bumpy halt. Bill West, driving the combine ignored them, but Wally Charman, standing on the bagging platform, waved. He paused to wipe his face. I was close enough to see the dust smear across his sun-reddened forehead. His burned forearms glowed below his rolled up shirtsleeves. None of the workers were stupid enough to work the fields bare-chested. The wheat straw stems slashed bare flesh as easily as a cat's claw, and the sun beating down on them without any protective shade, would burn to blistering in less than an hour.

My straw hat dangled down my back on its elastic straps and it was a quick flick of one hand to rest it back on my head. I didn't like wearing hats, but having just suffered recurrent bouts of brucellosis, my weakened body would only succumb to blinding headaches if I allowed the sun to beat down on my unprotected scalp.

I hopped down from the trailer, taking care to avoid the Mag-weeds, and watched the combine eating a path toward the remaining stand. Though I hated the thought, there was still a part of me that was compelled to witness the spectacle about to take place. Len, Andy, my father and the rest were lining up level with the machine, ready to bag their knockings. As the harvester's blades bit into the wheat stems a rabbit bolted out from a few feet beyond them. Then another, and another. Several pigeons and then a hare. The men rushed forward with sticks and nets, shouting commands at each other that no one seemed to take heed of.

Wally lifted a .22 rifle from the side of the platform and let rip, its sharp crack not audible over the roaring of tractor and combine. He broke and reloaded with fluid ease and shouldered the rifle for another shot. I saw a fleeing rabbit tumble and lay still.

The combine crawled on, apparently oblivious to the gnat-swarm of hunters scrabbling for their prizes. The machine swung out from the end of the short sweep and lined up for the final cut. I held my breath. Most of the game would have gone by now, but I knew there would always be a last minute dash. The combine was coming toward me at an angle. The final stand was quivering before the machine's inexorable progress. And then, from the last eight feet of corn, a tiny roe deer leaped out into the gratten. It paused, confused by the noise and the smells of machine and man, and fled them, running almost directly toward me. I stood stock still, holding my breath, saw Wally raise the rifle and take aim, and lower it as he caught sight of me standing on the headland. The deer plunged into the hedge just twenty feet to my right, and was gone.

Len reached me first and looked through into the next field where the doe had last been. The quarry was gone. He looked at me in disgust. 'You could've yelled at it,' he said. 'Turned it away. Wally could've got a shot in. He couldn't while you were in the way.'

'Sorry,' I mumbled, though I was not. The deer sighting was a rare treat. Seldom did I get to see these shy animals so close, and the thought of killing them was abhorrent.

My father ran up to me and bent to envelop me in a bear-hug. 'You all right?' he asked. 'God, I thought ol'Wal was goowin t' shoot. He only just saw you.' He hugged me closer still. 'You should know not to get in range, Pet.'

'Sorry,' I repeated and struggled to release his hold that was beginning to stifle the breath from me. I managed to hold the trug a little higher and squeaked, 'I'll go'n get your sloes.'

He knelt to look me in the eyes, searching my face for who knew what damage. 'You'm all roight then?'

'I'm all right, Dad. Honest.' I gave him a brief hug in return. 'See you later.' I hesitated. 'Don't tell mum about Wally though. Please. She'll get all uppy.'

'I shall 'ave to, pet. You can bet half a dollar one o' them'll say something.'

'Maybe not.' I gave him a last hug and pushed through the hedge into Kiln Shaw. The cottage was in sight from here, just half way down the hill, and the hedge that ran toward it was full of sloes. I set to picking, determined to set the incident to one side. It was not as if I had been in real danger, I told myself, unlike the deer.

I had wanted to fill the small trug, but after picking all the riper fruit it was little more than half full and I realised my heart was not in it. Hunger gnawed at me, and I was tired, though I would not have admitted that to anyone. A few fields over I could hear the drone of tractors, and see the cloud of dust rising into the clear sky. I watched a pair of larks rising, lost in their song, until they were out of sight, and my belly added a fresh chorus of its own.

I headed for home.

'You're late,' Mother grumbled. 'And look at the state of you. Up to your eyes in mud again. And I've got to be back down the big-house in half an hour.'

I proffered the basket of sloes with a wide smile. 'Dad wanted these. I got enough. I think.'

Mother nodded, mollified. 'Well you'd better go straight up for a bath, or you won't have time to get down to the Hall, and I'm not having you go out in that state.'

I looked down at myself and sighed. I was not exactly clean, but on the other hand I didn't think I was that dirty either. But mothers always had a very different idea about what were acceptable levels of dust. I confined myself to a quiet 'Yes Mum.'

There was a bright side, because for once I would get the bath water first whilst it was still hot, and scum free. It annoyed me that I was often last in the queue. Mother's skewed logic was that as boys were dirtier they automatically required hotter water to get clean. But it meant that I often had to scrub in lukewarm scummy depths where my hand was lost to view three inches from the surface. As the hot water tank did not run to more than one filling of the bath in an evening there was no other choice except to bath in the sink. Being small for my age I had often been washed kitchen's huge stone sink, in full view of every one until well after my eighth birthday; much to my embarrassment.

I sidled out of the kitchen.

I didn't want Len's bath water after he'd been hefting dust-laden corn-sacks and straw all day. I also wanted to be out of the house before Mother got wind of the incident with the gun. I felt sure she would see it as some excuse to prevent my going out. I rushed toward the stairway door before anyone else figured that out.

'Not too much hot water,' my mother called after me. 'Other people're having baths tonight.'

Twenty minutes later, as I scrubbed my fingernails to remove every scrap of dirt, because Captain was sure to do an inspection, I wondered what dances the band would play. It wasn't like country dancing at school, I knew, but not so very different. I was sure to know some of them. It was the first Harvest Supper I had attended, an event that I was eagerly anticipating. But I would be going on my own. My mother was *Chapel* and so didn't attend church events, and my father and brother were still busy with the last of the harvest,

I was finding my first year at senior school a passport to a lot of other firsts. After school clubs, proper sports like netball and hockey, homework clubs; though I was not sure that was such a privilege. And now being allowed to cycle to Guides for my first Harvest Supper.

I leaned forward to pull out the bath plug and stood up to dry myself. I would need to hurry if I wanted to be at the hall by seven, and I still had to drop my stuff at Linda's on the way as I was staying over night with her.

I carefully dragged on my uniform and carefully-folded and knotted my carefully-ironed, pale yellow, tie the regulation three fingers width from my belt, and stood admiring my reflection in the age spotted mirror on my dressing table. I had stitched the white Seconder's stripe onto the breast pocket with my own hands, and if I was going to be critical the stitching was neither even, nor perfectly straight, but I was too proud of it to worry. I looped my brand-new Seconders' lanyard around my neck, clipped the end to my belt, and stood back to admire the full effect. I tugged at the dark-blue beret that never sat at quite the right angle on unruly curls, frowned slightly, and whipped it off again, stuffing it into the deep pocket of my stiff serge skirt. I'd sort it out when I arrived at the hall. Grabbing my bag I thundered down the stairs.

'I'm off now, Mum.'

'Okay then. Don't forget to give Mrs Hurst that sloe gin.' My mother packed a dark green wine bottle into my handlebar basket, and tutted, irritably as she wrestled to lodge the bottled fruit and the marrow in a hessian bag where they wouldn't fall out in a hurry.

I hid a smile as the marrow slewed to one side and then

picked it out and rammed it down the side of my satchel. 'No, Mum,' I smiled widely now. 'It don't fit.'

'Well mind you don't break it. It's very good of Mrs Hurst to have you, so mind you behave, and don't forget to say thank you.'

'What's that one for?' I asked as two more bottles were juggled into the space.

'That's elderberry wine for the punch. Alby asked your dad to send one so give that to him soon as you get to the hall. And the other is sloe gin, for Goody Hurst. All right?'

I nodded, and began to edge away. 'Gotta go now, Mum, or I'll be late.'

'And whose fault's that? Poking around in all the mud?' My Mother pursed her lips, but I could see it was only to hide a grin of her own. 'Go on with you. See you tomorrow. Have a good time and behave.'

'I will,' I managed a quick wave as she wobbled away. The heavy load in the basket made the journey down the track precarious and I was never more glad than when I finally pedalled onto the metalled surface of Brewhurst Road and started off toward the common. I was glad to be away, and glad not to have to spend an evening hiding the near miss from my mother, who was a worrier by nature; one who worried from the hip, firing off indiscriminately at any one she considered to be in the wrong.

I pushed the thought from my mind, and stood up on the pedals to gain speed. I was late, I knew that much when the light was fading already, and I hadn't got very good lamps on my bike. I hoped I'd get to Linda's before I ran into Mr Dyer. He had never stopped me, but he had confiscated Steve Jennings' bike just because he had no lights; or so rumour had it. Rumour also said that Steve had been weaving away from the Working Men's Club at the time.

When I reached the Hurst's house there was no one home. I was a lot later than I had meant to be. That was a black mark with Captain, maybe even losing a patrol point. Not a good start to my Patrol Seconder status.

Dumping everything I didn't need for the evening ahead in the woodshed, I pedalled on toward the Village Hall as fast as I was able whilst still laden with jars and bottles and giant marrows.

Evening was closing in, but it was not yet past dusk and as I hurried into the mud and gravel entrance to the hall an owl sounded from close by. I parked my bike in the rack and gathered up my contribution to the supper. The owl sounded again. I glanced around me; cautious. It wasn't unknown for owls to be about this early on a fine evening but these seemed somehow different.

A rustle in the privet at the back of the racks drew my attention but I managed not to turn my head in response. The owl sounded once more. I smiled. Now that I was actively listening I could tell that this was no owl of the feathered kind. This sound was made through a grass stem; held, I had no doubt, between the thumbs of one Linda Hurst.

I hauled my bags toward the entrance doors, and braced myself. Sure enough, as I reached a hand toward dark-stained hall doors a whisper of gravel sounded behind me and I was 'tagged' roughly on the shoulder.

'You're late.'

'I know. I had to get dad some sloes.' I grinned at Linda, returning the punch and jerking back to avoid a second round.

'Captain's not happy.'

I shrugged. 'Can't 'elp that can I?'

'No,' Linda agreed. 'What ya got?'

'Marr'ers. Pears an' some elderberry wine for the punch.'

'Better hurry up then. Mr Charman's makin' the punch now.'

'Right,' I said, and pushed through into the hall to set some of my baggage down near the stage among the harvest festival goods.

'I brought some carrots, and our Jackie made two cakes,' Linda pointed out her family's contributions. 'And Goody

Hurst brought some ginger pop for us to drink with our dinner. It's in the kitchen. Speaking of which I'm on veg duty,' Linda sighed and turned away. 'Better get back to peeling. See you later?'

Linda had already dived into the melee that was the village hall before I could reply. The space was alive with people rushing in erratic dashes from one end to the other. To the untrained eye it could have looked like a rather disorganised British Bulldog match. The noise was positively ear-ringing in the vast, high roofed and wood-floored room. Even with tables and chairs and people to deaden the echo it was still a rattling room that swallowed crowds wholesale. With the added clatter of plates being unpacked and stacked, piles of chairs being dragged into rows on either side of the tables, rushing feet clattering, voices raised ever louder to compete with the hubbub; it was like walking into a tangible mass of sound.

The Hall was almost unrecognisable as the barren space in which we had our weekly Guide meetings. Sheaves of corn were tied in every corner and from every beam. Garlands of small branches and flowers were being looped around the walls and across the front of the stage that was already twined with flags and bunting and paper decorations. Most of the stage was heaped with produce that would be carried in procession to the church for Harvest Service the next morning. The rest of the stage was set aside for the musicians that would play for the dancers when supper was cleared away.

I stood for a moment, wondering what to do first.

'Ah, Susan. You finally made it then?'

'Sorry I'm late, Captain. My Dad asked me to get'n pick some sloes afore I came out.'

Our Guide Captain, Barbara Harris, nodded. 'A hand's turn's never a waste,' she observed. 'But we're behind. Can you help Tina setting cutlery?'

'Yes, Captain.' I sidled along the rows of trestle tables covered in snowy cloths and grabbed a handful of forks from my patrol leader, Tina Willis.

'You're late,' said Tina.

I nodded. It hardly seemed worth answering and I had the distinct feeling that if I had it would not be the answer that Tina expected, or wanted. On the whole, it seemed wiser to say nothing.

'Yer, Maid.'

The voice was unmistakable. To hear it raised was unusual, however. I turned toward Alby.

'Where's they wine your ol' man promised me, then?' Alby bellowed.

'On the stage,' I called back. 'In they sackin' bag with the marrow.'

I went back to my fork laying, carefully placing out a large and small fork by each plate, while Tina followed with knives and spoons. We had almost finished when Mrs Melton began rearranging them from the other side of the table.

'This is all completely wrong, girls. Has no one taught you anything?' She snatched another pair of carefully positioned spoons and forks at the top of the setting and laid them between the knife and fork. 'Start at the outside.' She laid a soupspoon on the right, and stepped back to look at it critically. 'And work your way in,' she added. 'You do not place dessert spoons at the top of the setting.'

'Why not?' I asked.

'Because, my dear, it's common.'

Tina and I looked at each other, confused by this sudden directive.

'But Captain said...' Tina began.

'Captain should know better. Heavens above. It isn't hard.'

'Problem, girls?' The Captain, swooped into our midst, cutting Meryl Melton off from the tables.

'Not at all, Barbara. I was just giving these girls some lessons on the correct rules of hostessing.' She smiled mechanically. 'Such a shame to see young girls so lacking in social skills. I suppose it comes from their rural upbringing.'

'Probably,' Mrs Harris was one of the old school; all tweeds and spaniels. An 'Honourable' as her cleaning lady, Iris West, was often heard to boast. Captain Harris favoured Mrs Melton with on of her most withering stares.

Mrs Melton took a step back, but jutted her chin defiantly. 'Well, we really should be setting an example Barbara.'

'No, Meryl, we are setting a table. And my girls are doing so according to local custom. Country custom.' She smiled with her mouth; the kind of smile that only paid service to civility in its strictest sense. 'You haven't lived here long have you, my dear? It may only be forty miles from London but its a million miles from The Ritz. You really should relax a little more. The whole idea of leaving London is get away from all that stress.' She gestured at the table. 'Carry on girls. You're doing a wonderful job. Now Meryl, perhaps you could help Mr Charman with the punch?' She led the beetroot shaded and trembling Mrs Melton toward the kitchen.

'Good job Cap's got eyes in 'er arse,' said Tina.

'I know.' I replied. 'I wonder what Alby'll make of 'er. If she tries to poke around in his punch I reck'n ee'll shove one of his ferrets up her corset.'

Tina shook her head. 'Nah, Mr Charman loikes 'is ferrets.'

We both giggled, but hurried to finish our task. Captain's glare could always be felt, on target and on time, from across the most crowded of rooms.

With the cutlery sorted we looked out the rest of the patrol and began laying the table decorations. Wheat sheaves sculpted in bread, corn dollies, crackers, hats, bowls of nuts and fruits and candles stuck in a variety of holders from old bottles to elegant brass sticks.

Tina stood back and surveyed our work with a grin. 'Tain't bad.' She said. 'I reck'n my old mam couldn't do it any better.

I nodded agreement. Tina's mother was housekeeper at the Grange, and treasured by the Colonel and his wife for her prowess in both kitchen and dining room, and Tina had learned much from helping her. More, I was willing to bet, than the incoming Londoner, Mrs Melton, and her ilk, that had lately begun to invade the village's new housing estates.

'So what now?' I asked.

Tina spread her hands. 'Not a lot. We were only down for tables. And we got it done quicker'n Captain thought. So,' she jerked her head toward the door. 'I reck'n we've about due fer a rest.'

'Right.'

We sidled toward the door, collecting the rest of the patrol on the way, and escaped before Captain could find us another job.

'What are we doing at tables tonight?' I said.

The five of us sat on the handrail bar of the 'witches hat' roundabout, that was made from a cone of iron poles attached to a pole at the top and to a circle of wood planks some two feet from the ground, at the bottom. We were all facing each other, our legs dangled in the centre of the ring, and Tina, as the tallest and therefore possessed of the longest legs, was periodically pushing off from the central pole to send the hat on an erratic ellipse.

The orange glow of sunset was almost gone, and we could not see each other's faces too clearly in the gloom. But I could imagine Tina's furrowed forehead as she gave the question some thought.

'Well, last year each patrol got a set of tables,' she replied. 'We've got five patrols, an' twenty tables, plus the head table.' She shrugged lightly. 'Shouldn't be too 'ard. Provided,' she leaned into the circle and glared around her, 'provided no one goes'n tips no dinners down no necks.'

'No, Tina.' The reply was prompt and almost in unison. Tina was not known for her forbearance and any patrol member who messed up in any way and lost Scarlet Pimpernel patrol points in any shape or form would find her retribution was both swift and painful.

'Teams?' I suggested.

Tina nodded. 'You take Lynn and, and I'll take Bev and

Jane.'

'That's fine.' I didn't mind being a small team of two against Tina's three. Lynn was a strapping lass that could carry twice as much as me. Bev and Jane, though keen and bright, were both fresh up from Brownies.

'Roight then, that's settled,' Tina said.

'Whilst it's very nice to hear you girls having a tactical meeting, there's work to be done inside.' Captain voice was close in the dark that had come quickly to the 'Rec' at the back of the hall.

'Sorry Captain.' Tina slid through the bars and grabbed the seats to bring the rocking to a halt so that the small ones could get off. Lynn and I just jumped. 'What do you want us to do?'

'The guests are arriving, so I want you girls to start in the kitchen with serving the drinks.'

'Yes, Captain.' We streamed inside, eager for something to do.

In the short space of time we had been behind the hall it had transformed from a seething chaos to a corn strewn grotto. The beams above the tables dripped greenery and bunting, there was barely an inch of wall that wasn't covered in sheaves or greens or yet more bunting, and the tables were as near to perfect as any could wish. Both Tina and I paused for a moment to admire our work before we dashed to the kitchen serving hatch.

Alby was already there and ladling punch into tiny glasses. 'Where 'av you maids bin?' he asked. 'I've bin dolloping the lot on me own.'

'Sorry Mr Charman. We didn't know we were on the drinks rota,' Tina replied. She grabbed a jug of squash and began pouring it into coloured metallic beakers borrowed from the school canteen.

We were not really busy with few people in the hall, beyond the Guides and a few adults, who that early in the evening preferred squash to either Alby's infamous punch, or a sample from the keg of Old Ale perched on the end of the counter.

'Good drop o' stuff, Alby,' Goody Hurst declared as she took a large sip from her second cup of punch. 'You've done yerself proud, bwoy.'

Alby nodded. 'Good thing I made double lots. Stan sent me up two bottles o' elderberry, so I sez to meself, why not?'

I paused mid-pour and stared at Alby. 'I only brought one bottle of elder,' I whispered to Tina.'

'He must've bin seein' double afore he started then,' Tina replied.

I shook my head. 'No. I had two bottles, But one of 'em were Sloe Gin.'

'Same colour,' Tina replied.

'Different taste,' I said, and realised Goody Hurst was watching us. I flushed and continued pouring.

Goody Hurst came to lean over the counter, her eyes were twinkling in fun, and whispered, 'Never mind, pet. I won't tell, if'n you won't.' She chuckled quietly. 'Oh, don't you go worrittin' about Ginny's gin. I shall tell 'er what 'appened. She likes a good larf.' She jerked her head toward the tables where several local dignitaries and would-be's were gathered at the top table. 'We shall 'ave a good larf, too. If that lot get's wound into that they punch.'

She glided away to her seat, still chortling to herself, and I thought little more of it until much later; except to wonder at the opening doors that going to 'big school' had shown me; insights into the adult world that had never been hinted at until I had left the village school. The half way house of double figure birthdays was an eye opener, and I found it very much to my taste on the whole.

The dinner was demolished as rapidly as the Guides could serve it, and the speech was a short one from the Chairman, who, this year, was Sid Grinstead. The Guides hurried to eat their own supper as the chairs were cleared for the proper part of the evening that every one was waiting for.

'Yer,' Linda handed a bottle of ginger beer to each of us.

'Gran made it. We c'n share a bottle now, and we've still got another four fer later on.'

'Ta,' Tina grabbed the bottle eagerly.

Linda backed away, warily. 'Careful. Don't shake it. It'll go of in yer 'and.'

She was smiling but I knew from experience she was only half joking. I had seen corks from Goody Hurst's ginger pop travel the length of her back yard if it was not treated with due respect.

I watched Tina open it very gently, easing the cork so that it fizzed its worst before she poured it out. The dinner was good, and better for Goody Hurst's gift.

Once supper was over we set our plates on the worktop in the kitchen. Orchid Patrol had drawn the short straw for washing up duty and now that the serving was over both Pimpernels' and Linda's Thistle patrol were free to enjoy what was left of the evening.

We all crowded into the hall just as the band had mounted the stage and begun the first reel. I soon found myself swept up into a melee of dancing of a kind that I never knew existed. This was not the ordered Thursday afternoon dance lessons from junior school days, just a few short months and a life time past. None of the stopping and starting that went on as the teacher corrected and cajoled all of the left-footed pupils into some semblance of order. This was dancing as I had always felt it should be.

There was laughter and exuberance, and the occasional tangle as someone or other misheard the caller and went the wrong way round, piling the dancers into domino heaps. The dancers danced and musicians played, and the beer and cider and punch, among the adults at least, flowed freely.

It was not long before even I, who was not used to excesses of any nature, realised that some people were much the worse for drink. I watched in undisguised glee Mrs Melton weaved her unsteady, punch inspired, path around the *Virginia Reel*, and whooped with laughter with all the rest as she finally came to a halt and slowly sank floor-wards in the middle of *Brighton Camp*.

'Sloe's'll do that to you, pet,' Goody Hurst said to me. 'Watch and learn, maid. Always know when you're runnin' on fumes. Nothin' wrong with a liddle drink. It keeps yer heart strong. But there's nuthin' worse than a drunk fer lookin' a dammed fool.'

I watched and had to agree. There was a world of difference between drink loosened laughter and drunken belligerence.

Mrs Melton was whirling among the sets in complete oblivion of her state. She was calling dance steps all of her own. 'Pair, swing, arch and parry. Swing your partners ... weeeeeeh!' she grabbed hold of Jimmy Shotter and whirled him around, until she staggered and fell. The drink was hurrying her brain, but her legs were not keeping up. She lay on the floor, still shouting orders, her dress ruched up around her thighs to display a pasty expanse of leg above her sagging stocking tops. 'Swing, parry, form an arch – come on. Where's that damned arch, you bloody bumpkins. Can't'cha even dance like real humans?'

The music had rumbled to a halt and the attention of the entire hall was focussed on the sprawled body in the centre of the floor. I looked around the circle and was amazed at the span of emotions written on the faces that were turned toward the prone woman. Amusement in most, embarrassment from some, especially those who had thought of her as friend, disgust mixed with a large measure of righteous disapproval from the older villagers. I had the distinct impression it was more to do with who than what. Had it been a local the comments would have been both ribald and heckling. As it was one of the 'nobs from The Avenue' there was a massed unease throughout.

'We can all dance, Meryl,' Captain stepped forward and hauled her to her feet. 'Except for you in that state. Time you went home, my dear.' She was smiling, but I could recognise the inflection on the last words. Captain was in the mood to hang, draw and quarter. 'Audrey? Would you?' She looked meaningfully at Audrey Miller, Meryl's neighbour on the new estate.

'Oh, yes,' Audrey rushed forward and took Meryl under the arm, her husband moving to grab the other.

As she was helped to the door there were few who didn't hear a comment that echoed all the thoughts of tutting matriarchs. Goody Hurst was heard to whisper, loudly, 'Them townies is all the same. Can't hold their drink. Disgracin' 'emselves somethin' awful.' There was a general titter of amusement from the locals.

I glanced around, wondering where I fitted in. I was local, born and bred, but my parents were relatively new. I caught a wink form Goody Hurst and relaxed. I had the seal of approval. None would question me whilst I stood under Goody Hurst's watching eye.

'G'night,' Mrs Melton called from the door, as she was half carried away. 'Good dance. Good dance. Awf'ly kind, and all that. Ta tah, chaps.'

The door swung closed behind her. A few more in-comers shuffled nervously as they scented the pack closing in on them. They were not exactly unwelcome as a general rule but it was obvious from the stern glances and whispered asides that all incomers were being linked with the odious Mrs Melton by default. There was a small silence and a few more un-locals sidled out of the hall.

The band tuned up idly, waiting for the doors to open and close on those who wished to depart, and then began to play a quiet, slow version of *Strip The Willow*. New rows of dancers hurried to form. I grabbed Linda and we took our places on the crowded floor.

It was a rowdy and long dance that took us at least twice around the sets. We stepped and skipped and swung with gusto, then fell into chairs after the final chord as exhausted as the rest. The band went on playing, but few got up to dance.

Instead the men began to gather around the kitchen hatch.

'Turn the cup over then, Alb.' Goody Hurst Called.

'I will d'reckly, woman.' He replied. 'Drink yer punch and 'ush now.'

Goody Hurst laughed and raised her glass, full of red liquid toward the light that glowed a ruby fire through the bowl. 'Good 'ealth, my ducks. And may the ploughshares never rust!'

'Ploughshares!' The toast rattled round the room. And Alby took off his hat and cradled a large cow horn of ale on the middle.

'Come on Wally,' he said. 'Turn it over lad.' And he began to sing, with just one fiddle accompanying him.

I've bin to Plymouth and I've bin to Dover
I have bin rambling, boys, all the world over,
Over and over and over and over
Drink up your liquor and turn your cup over
Over and over and over and over
The liquor's drink'd up and the cup is turned over.

As he sang, with the gathered crowd joining in a ragged chorus Wally picked up the cap, balancing the horn in its centre and began to drink. Tipping his lined throat back to let the liquid run freely down his gullet in a smooth flood.

As he grabbed the horn and slapped on the counter, I could now see that the point of the horn cup was tipped with metal, and the drinking edge rimmed with similar material. Whether silver or pewter I could not tell. From both ends was looped a ragged red chord by which, I assumed, it would be hung when not in use. Polished and scrubbed with years of use, it was old. How old I could not begin to guess.

A large cheer went up as Wally looked around him. He pointed at Barry Charman. 'You, bwoy.'

Barry stepped forward, and the chant went up with a recharged glass. Barry finished with a flourish and slapped the glass down, pointing at Tim Ralph as he did so. And so it went on. The glass turning over and over and over. Those that could not clear the glass in the space of the verse were charged a fresh glass and kept trying until they could, or else collapsed in the attempt.

I watched, fascinated. This was a new facet of adult life that I had never imagined existed. My teetotal mother would never have allowed me to come had she suspected such a practise. I wondered that my father had allowed it, but I knew he was not averse to me having a glass or two of wine, and he knew I was watched over by Goody Hurst in my every move.

The band played on, and a few dancers danced as the rowdy drinkers carried on their ancient game. I had no doubt it was ancient. There was something about it all that seemed rather like the Viking lifestyle I'd been studying in history.

Except that Vikings had never had cannons, or guns of any description that I had learned of thus far. It was something like a cannon that exploded somewhere near the back of the hall.

The band halted abruptly, and the dancers stopped dead in their tracks. All attention turned beyond the drinkers to the kitchen area.

The moment's silence was broken by a loud guffaw. 'Yer, Goody Hurst.' Wally shouted. 'What're you puttin' in they bottles of pop? Baggerin things're goin' up, loike 'and gr'nades.'

The tension burst, as easily as the dark brown bottles of ginger pop, and a growing barrage of laughter rippled through the gathering.

'Pop's the word, eh? Goody Hurst?' Tim called. He peered cautiously through the hatch. 'Bloody good job there weresn't no one in there. Tis a bloody mess, I c'n tell yer.' He leaned in a little further. 'Ow many bottles did you 'ave?'

'I brung arf a dozen,' Goody Hurst bustled to the head of the crowd and peeped over the counter. 'Ow many 'ave you 'ad, young Linda?'

'Two,' Linda replied. 'I put en by the sink in a bucket o'

cold water.'

'Oh.' They turned to the Captain who was, for the first time I could recall, actually at a loss. 'I emptied it out and put them on the floor by the ovens. They were in the way.'

'So they'm bin warmin' up nice?' Tim nodded curtly, and leaned in as far as he could. 'I c'n see two left standin'. He slid back to the floor and looked around him, frowning. 'What'cha reck'n, Ro?'

The Roland Dyer, village policeman, took a quick look at the carnage that had been the hall's kitchen. 'Well. I think it's a call for the bomb squad,' he said.

'Roight,' Tim said, sarcastic. 'Goody Hurst's pop. The latest deadly weapon.'

'It's a lethal one,' Ro replied. He scratched his chin and shrugged. 'Tell you what. I'll ring the Sarg first. But I'll have to close the hall down. Sorry folks. It's too dangerous with all that glass flying about.' He turned to the crowd and raised his voice. 'Sorry. But I shall have to ask you to all go home. And no one's to go through that kitchen until it's been made safe.'

'Flippen 'eck,' Linda muttered. 'That's gotta be a first. Harvest supper closed for a ginger pop alert.'

'Goody Hurst strikes again,' I replied.

We followed the crowd out into the hall's car park. People milled around, chattering excitedly. Few showed any signs of actually heading for their beds. Only those with children reluctantly ushered their offspring away. It was a warm night. The stars bright in a moonless sky. We headed for the swings whilst we waited for Goody Hurst and Ginny.

'Bomb squad?' I said. 'Wonder how long that will take.'

'Hours,' Linda replied. 'Unless the local Terriers 've got a depot with the right people.'

I nodded. Linda would know, with her father being in the reserves. 'Reck'n we'll get to see it all?'

'Doubt it,' she grinned suddenly. 'But who cares? It's not a Harvest Supper any one'll forget in a hurry.'

Elderberry Wine

8 lb elderberries

1 gall water

3 lb Demerara sugar

½ teaspoon whole allspice

1 teaspoon cloves

1 oz ground ginger

1 oz yeast

Slice of toast

Method

1. Strip berries from stalks and mash them well in a crock.

2. Cover them with the water and leave for several days, stirring each day to extract the juice, stirring every day.

3. Strain the mixture into a preserving pan, add the sugar and dissolve it.

4. Add spices and boil for half an hour.

5. Cool and strain back into the crock.

6. Spread toast with the yeast and float it on the surface.

7. Leave to ferment for a week, stirring daily.

8. Skim, strain off into a demijohn with a fermentation lock.

9. Leave until fermented out. When fermentation is finished bottle and store for minimum of six months.

Sloe Gin (or vodka)

1. Half fill a Kilner jar with washed, pricked sloes.

2. Add four ounces of castor sugar and fill jar to the top with gin.

3. Screw the lid on tight.

4. Shake the jar ever day until the sugar is dissolved and the liquid is a dark colour. Half a teaspoon of almond essence can be added after two weeks.

5. Leave for two months, shaking often.

6. Run the liquid through a double muslin several times to remove all particles which would otherwise spoil the clarity.

7. Store in half sized liqueur bottles.

Note: this method can be used with all manner of firm berry-type fruit, including cherries, blueberries, blackcurrants, rosehips etc. If, like me, you do not like the perfumed smell of gin then use vodka, (blueberry vodka is especially good). I have also known people to use sloe wine and mix half wine/half gin, but this does not keep as well, and does not have the same kick. I was always told that you should only ever use a silver fork to prick the fruit as silver would not 'taste'. As I don't possess any silver cutlery I have always used a stainless steel fork and had no problems to date.

Medicinal – Elderberry

Elder is possibly one of the most widely used plants, and all of the plant is used for almost all parts of the body – from head to toe.

Elderberry wine is said to be an aid against pain in childbirth. It is also good for stomach complaints and as a method of reducing inflammation, especially in the case of arthritic joints etc. Warmed with a little cinnamon elderberry wine eases colds and flu. It is also good for asthma, sciatica, neuralgia and toothache.

Elderberry syrup also eases coughs and colds. A traditional Sussex cure for whooping cough consisted of dried and crushed elderberries mixed with common salt and live snails freshly removed from their shells; and before you ask, no, I haven't tried it.

Berries fried with mutton fat could cure boils and ulcers.

Dried berries can be infused in boiling water, strained and a little honey added to relieve phlegmy coughs.

Elderberries can be an efficient laxative and diuretic as well as kidney and lung tonic.

Elderfire is made from elderberries and whisky in the same way you make sloe gin and is mixed with boiling water and honey to ease coughs and flu.

Infusions of elderberries or flowers can be used for headaches and other minor pains.

It also said to help with epilepsy and seizures.

Elderflower ointment is a good cure for warts.

An infusion of elderflowers, as a wash or in an ointment, will alleviate piles.

A compress of elderflowers can be used on minor burns or inflamed or itching eyes. Elderflower water makes a good eyewash for tired eyes.

Boil the elderflowers in borage water and drink a glassful every morning for youthful skin (about one tablespoon dry flowers to a pint of water)

Macerated leaves and flowers in mutton fat make a good complexion cream.

For painful feet boil elder bark in salt water and use as a lotion.

Water in which elder roots have been boiled is said to relieve rheumatic pain.

The pith of elder contains a mild sedative/sleeping draught.

Note: all of the above medicinal uses apply only to British elder. American elder is *toxic* and though this toxicity lessens in drying it should not be used unsupervised, especially on children.

Medicinal – Sloes

The bitter sloes (or blackthorns) have been used to treat stomach ailments (flowers to lessen, fruits to bind).

Note: take care with sloes (in or out of vodka) if you are on any medication.

Traditional – Elderberry

Elder (also known as Bour or Boor) was always seen as a death tree and was often planted at burial sites.

It was also known as both a Witch tree and Fairy tree and in consequence was thought to be protected by them.

It was thought that the Queen of Elves lived in the roots of the elder.

To cut down elder could result in bad luck, or even death.

Gertrude Jekyll the famous garden designer said that elder planted near a well tainted the water.

It was said you should not use elder to repair fences as it let witches and fairies in at your livestock.

Elder could not be burned in or even enter, the house

In Ireland it was said that any family that allowed elder to thrive on its property would die out.

There are numerous traditions of evil and witchery attached the 'Old Woman' as the elder was often known. Perhaps this is because it was associated with the Crone aspect of the Goddess because of its medicinal properties.

Snakes have often been found among the roots, probably because of the dry shelter they provide.

Whatever the reason, for every tale of evil and woe another tells of protection and good health.

Sprigs of elder were often tucked into hats and harness to relieve both driver and horse from the attentions of insects. Flies and midges avoid the rank smelling leaves. Indeed Elder was often planted near dairies and alike for this reason.

A twig carried in the pocket would protect a rider from saddle sores.

If dew soaked leaves were strewn in a flea infested room the fleas would stick to the leaves and die.

Dipped in oil and floated in a bowl of water elder sticks can make reasonable candles.

At the Rollright Stones in Oxfordshire it was traditional on Midsummer Eve to gather round the King Stone and cut the elder flowers around the stones – and when this was done the King Stone would move his head. This arises from the legend that a Danish King and his army going to battle for the English crown asked a Witch associated with Mother Elder what his fate should be. She tricked him, and turned the King and his army into stones, thus preventing them from going into battle. The stone circle is still surrounded by elders to this day.

Country folk were known to smoke elder leaves when tobacco was not available (or affordable), and was often said to be preferred. As Withering (1776) reported, the plant should be avoided, and not slept under or near, due to its narcotic smell, I wonder if this was not truer than they realised.

Elder is also said to be the tree on which Judas Iscariot hung himself, and this is why it has such an offensive (and, according to some, even poisonous) smell, and the berries are so small and sour, having shrivelled from the shame.

Cutting elder was not a problem in many areas provided the tree's permission was asked first.

In the south it was thought that elder was a warmer wood than most because it flowered near the solstice – and was a favoured wood for shelves and perches in henhouses.

Elder was planted deliberately next to houses to protect the occupants from witches or from evil spirits and lightening strike. In some areas the protection only worked if a rowan was planted with the elder.

Hollowed out, the stems were used to make flutes, blowpipes and it was even known for thick enough stems to be filled with melted lead and used as a walking stick/ weapon.

Traditional – Sloes

Other than that most references to blackthorns are as a witches' tree and as late as the 1940s anyone seen to carry a blackthorn walking stick was suspected of being a witch; for example such a stick pointed at a pregnant women or animal could cause immediate miscarriage.

In a direct contradiction to this there are many instances of a blackthorn staff being carried as a badge of civic office eg Sandwich, Kent.

Blackthorn is considered to be an unlucky plant to bring indoors as has occurred with many trees and plants associated with the old religion. Many believe this may have been as much to disassociate people from old habits and beliefs as to any real threat to well being.

Shillelaghs, the traditional Irish walking sticks often cited as weapons of choice, are made from blackthorn.

As a pagan plant is was considered to be good luck. At the New Year, a globe constructed from its branches was burned and scattered among furrows of early crops to 'drive the demons from the field' and to ensure a good harvest.

A new globe or wreath was then made by the women and hung in the kitchen until the following New Year.

The flowering of blackthorn in April or May often coincides with a frosty spell – hence the term 'blackthorn winter'.

It was said that planting of barley crops was best done when the blackthorn was in full bloom.

Blackthorn berry juice was used as an inking dye to put patterns onto cloth (if you have ever spilled the juice you will know what an effective dye it is).

They have culinary uses for jellies and jams and cordials as well as wines.

In certain parts of Ireland the leaves were sometimes used as a substitute for tobacco.

Parz'mut Whisky & Wurzel Wine

My mother was an efficient if unimaginative cook. It was not something she enjoyed doing and she did not appreciate people being 'under her feet'. She bustled from table to oven to pantry as she cooked for the evening's repast and the family found it was best to be absent altogether when the kitchen was really busy.

I frequently opted for helping my father in whatever he was doing that day, even though helping often involved sitting around watching whilst he worked. On one particular day the task at hand was loading a cart with mangold wurzels from a pile steeped high against the far wall of the Sussex barn. It was something I could at least make a token effort at, I was not worried about working but I was just not a domestic creature and despite poor health much preferred being up to my ears in muck to wielding brooms and washing up.

We had finished sorting a pile of beet veg and were waiting for Wally and Alby Charman to bring a cart up to the barns for loading, but the Charmans were late, and after spending an hour or more standing on the metal five-bar gate, straining for a first view of the cart, I had almost decided to go home.

The communal bonfire celebrations were looming closer by the hour and I had offered to help my father because I knew it was better to keep busy as it seemed to make time hurry along. This particular job wasn't one I found that interesting, and after shovelling root veg for an hour or so I was more than ready to do something, anything, else … but Mother was in the kitchen. The choices were hard.

I stood on my toes and craned my neck for a view further than the first corner of the track. There was not a great deal to see at this end of the lane. There, where it had passed the farm, and our home, passed the lambing sheds, passed the Colonel's country house, and then on to the barns that stood in the middle of the top field, the lane was little more than a mud track with grass growing between twin lines ploughed into it by tractor tyres. Once, the lane had continued over the hill, down to the river and across to the mill. A weir had replaced the bridge many years ago and it was no longer passable for vehicles, and no one ever went that way on foot, bar the odd hiker.

Newfarm Lane saw few passers-by only the occasional parties of ramblers on a Sunday afternoon and the inevitable stoic fisherman or two headed for the weir. NO THROUGH ROAD said the sign where the lane met the Sayers Common Road, and it was no idle comment. Visitors were few and I made the most of what we had.

In the colder months when the Charman's tiny farm was not busy Wally Charman would cycle up the lane to help with sheep dipping, or hedging, or some other labour intensive task. And when our paths crossed, he would always say hello. More important, from my point of view, were the toffees that he kept in his pocket; toffees that he would unfailingly share, and in consequence I endeavoured to be in that *right time and place* as often as I could.

The lane's banks were topped with the towering remnants of parsley and willow herb that were now brown, lacking even the crystalline dusting of frost that they had worn in the earliest part of the day. Wally's cloth cap, bobbing and lurching between those banks, was the first hint of his arrival. I stretched up on tip-toe to make sure that is was, indeed, Wally and not some other elderly gent that had strayed into the lane, though one cloth cap was very like another at that distance. The sounds of horses' hooves and harness and the rumble of cartwheels on the rough ground came clearly through the quiet afternoon, and with it Wally's habitual tuneless whistling, which came in curious bursts of sound and rhythm that coincided with the ruts and bumps of the lane.

The cart had turned the corner now, and I could see the carter's weathered face was red from exertion, long streams of mist streaming from his pursed lips.

Except that it was not Wally, but his father Alby. It mattered not to me. Alby was as good for a toffee as his boy. Like father, like son, as my gran would say.

Alby was drawing level with us and brought the cart to a halt. The whistling stopped as he began to dismount. He was wheezing loudly from the effort. He was not a young man. Wally seemed old to me, far older than my father, which made Alby a veritable ancient. His thin face was a filigree of lines, with all of his features succumbing to the rules of gravity, giving him a look somewhere between tortoise and bloodhound; his head seemed sunken between his shoulders, his hands lumpen and overlarge and his legs, when he alighted, were bowed to such an alarming degree that the old saying 'couldn't stop a pig in a passage' might have been invented with Alby in mind. He greeted my silent appraisal with a quiet, 'Morn'n maid.'

'Allo, Mr Charman,' I said again, demure, my face wreathed in innocent smiles. I stepped down from the gate and danced up to greet him, making sure to give his horse, the unpredictable Dolly, a wide berth. I liked horses, and on another day would have made a fuss of her, but having no apples to offer it was safer to let her crunch the *snaffle* around her mouth in peace. I knew from bitter experience how she could use those long, yellowed teeth to exact quick and painful retribution if the tidbits she felt you must surely have were withheld.

'Cold, innit?' Alby rummaged in his right hand pocket for a handkerchief to wipe moisture from his nose and nodded to my father with a slightly louder, 'Marnin' Stan.' His other hand slid into the left pocket of his jacket and he withdrew three gold-wrapped toffee pennies. He proffered one to me. 'Yer,' he said. 'Present for'e maid.'

'Thank you, Mr Charman.' I leaned forward to take one

toffee from his arthritis-cupped palm. There was apparent surprise in my voice, though it was a well-worn ritual, and neither of us was fooled by it. Alby flipped a second toffee penny to my father before slowly unwrapping his own; popping it into his mouth and chewing steadily, a slow smile on his lips.

He often told my father he liked me because, 'she do keep a civil tongue'; which went a long way in his book. When asked he excused the toffee treats he did not extend to Len because, he said, 'she be that windshaken. Any bit o'stuff won't go amiss. Build her up a bit. Right ampery maid she be,' I once overheard him say to his wife. 'Catched hot with the bangs she did, up at Callings Farm when she were a liddle'bab.' I hated being spoken of like a toddler, but knew my semi-invalid status made me somehow *more tender* than my years in many eyes, particularly older country men. This was doubtless because they had long memories of siblings, and perhaps even their own children, who had not come through such events. I knew they all felt pity for me and it was a situation I bore as gracefully as I could, and with all the ruthlessness of youth had no qualms in playing on those fears when there were toffees at stake. Now that I was at secondary school I had an idea my toffee-days were nearing an end.

I followed the men into the barn, with its interior that remained cool in summer and warm on winter mornings and was always dingy. The high windows were obscured by hay, cobwebs, and a half-century's dust, so that the only light of any use trickled through the double-doors through which the cart would come.

During November the top of the stack still rose high among the rough-hewn roof beams. Hundreds of bales, ready to be strewn as winter bedding for the livestock. I usually climbed to the top because it offered me the best view of the barn's interior, with the added advantage of sharing it with a half-dozen spitting, snarling farm cats that my mother would never allow as pets, no matter how I begged to be allowed to bring a kitten home.

That day, however, the furred harridans had vacated, annoyed that all hope of sleeping or ratting were gone as Alby's Scots-border collie, Badger, explored the hay loft's ample space with his grandson, our very own Bo. The two dogs snuffled and snorted around the loft, backing off now and again to sneeze before diving back in for more scrabbling and whining after rats that I had no doubt were too wily to be anywhere near them during daylight hours.

The air in the barn was laden with the unmistakable odours of dirt floor, hay-chaffs and mice, and yes, rats. I leaned out to peer at the workers below and to catch the cold breeze wafted from beyond the doors. Frost-tainted air coming with the late afternoon gloom. I breathed deep, closing my eyes in pleasure as it cleared the 'mildew and mouse' from my lungs.

Dolly stood dozing between the shafts, stirring a little as lumpy round mangolds begun hitting the backboard. She tossed her head to scatter a late cloud of midges. There were no sprigs of insect-repelling elder to hang from her head collar at this time of year and she shook her head, harness jingling, every few seconds under the insect onslaught that the sun brought, even on such a cold day as this.

The two men had paused, and reached for tobacco tins almost in unison.

'You going up the common tonight, Alby?' My father asked.

'Oh arr. I shall be there alroight. Never missed one yet.'

'Good. I hear David Corbett's got a good sized barrel of old jack.'

Alby nodded, grinning. 'He do be a man as grows stuff fer a living. Ee'd 'ave a good apple or two up there. And I knows fer a fact ee's got a 'alf dozen old cider apple trees there 'as 'is gaffer planted special.'

'So I hear.' Father pushed away from the cart. 'I'd best be getting along cos young Suzie up there's been raring to go all afternoon. Can't wait to see her pocket money go up in smoke.' He looked up at me, and I limited my reply to a poked-out tongue. 'See all the thanks I get?'

'Tis babs fer en, lad. Ain't none of 'em got a kind word fer their old man,' Alby replied. 'Any road. I'd best be orf an' all. Badgerrrrrrr!'

Needing no second summons Badger scrambled down the bales onto the cart, where he sat, bolt upright, expectant of his return to home and supper. 'Oi'll be orf then,' Alby wheezed, pulling himself on-board and untwisting the reins.

'Hang on a bit Alby.' My father turned to his coat, discarded on a stack of straw bales. He brought out a deep green bottle that bore a plain white label declaring the contents as PARSNIP – 1962. 'I haven't tried this one yet. Let us know what its like.'

'Parz'mut? Drop of good stuff, then.' Alby's eye twinkled impishly from a lean and lined face. 'Thankee lad. Oi shall 'ave a sup o' they when oi gets 'ome.' He touched his cap with one bent forefinger. 'See yer then bwoy,' and raising his voice to call out, 'even'n maid,' he flicked the reins sharply. 'C'mon Doll,' he chirped, 'shift yer arse, you lapsy old bagger.'

Dolly leaned into the harness and lurched forward. The load slid as the cart bumped over the ruts, but settled quickly, and carter, cart and horse were soon swallowed by the dusk that gathered early beneath the trees.

'Can we go now, Dad?' I demanded.

Dad laughed and ruffled my hair. 'I suppose so.'

I bore the ruffle without comment. Time with my father without any one else was special. And tonight we had a treat that was better still. Tonight, I reminded myself for the hundredth time, was Guy Fawkes.

The previous Saturday we had gone in to Guildford and I had spent a pleasing half hour choosing fireworks whilst Len got cross. He had taken less than five minutes to buy a box of bangers, two rockets and a bag of jumping jacks. I was not so easily swayed. I took time to consider the merits of each gaudily wrapped tube and cone. When younger I had preferred the Roman Candles, or a packet of hand-helds with wooden handles and tantalising names; Golden Flowers or Jack and Jills. Or else packets of sparklers, plain white ones in dozens and in half dozens for coloured. Now I leaned toward Traffic Lights, Screech Owls, or rockets in all sizes. So many to choose from and only three and nine pence to spend.

Len would already be up at the Corbett's nursery, helping to build the bonfire and our mother would be with her friend, Mrs Corbett, setting out treacle toffee, sausage rolls, ginger parkin and glazed apples for the neighbourhood to feast on when they gathered for the evening. It was a bigger social event than Christmas. One where all of the locals in that end of the Common had an out-door party.

The frost was well on its way by the time my father and I had gone home to wash, change and walked the mile and a half across the common to the Corbett's lower field.

In the spring and summer that field was a mass of spring blooms grown for Guildford flower market, but from the 'hunter's moon' to the 'cold' it was just a ploughed field. And rock solid it was, with frost working deep into weald clay, so that the warps and furrows were hard on the ankles. I clutched my brown paper bag of fireworks close, treating it with the tenderness I would give a parcel of eggs as I trudged behind my father, tripping every few yards on another ridge of solidified soil. I would not be sorry to arrive.

It was dark, with sprinklings of stars dotting a clear sky. The moon was just up, wearing the misty blue/white skirt around its edges that spoke of a hard frost. Blades of grass that I could see in the torchlight were already glistening with feathery edges of solidifying moisture.

Before us, rising over the top of the immediate horizon, sat the tower of wood that had been weeks in the building. It was over twelve feet high, and at its top perched the 'guy'; a shadowed figure, barely to be seen against the sky, lit by wavering torches held by those below. Now and then a beam would slide across the effigy, lighting its Wurzel head, left over from Punkie Night the week before. In that faint light it was almost too real. I felt a small thrill skitter down my spine, and a little anger at the same time. Len had cycled the three miles into the village to parade the Punkie lanterns from house to house with the scouts, but I had not been allowed.

'Too far and too cold,' my mother had declared. 'You've been poorly.'

Quite a large crowd had gathered already, and more people were sauntering in from all directions.

I hurried forward to hand Mr Corbett the brown paper bag of goodies, almost falling into him in my haste. He took it, laughing. 'Easy on there. They won't run away just yet.' He lifted the lid on a wood chest and laid my offerings among the cache of delights, which I only glimpsed in awe before he closed the lid again.

'Keep 'em safe,' he said. 'We'll be lighting the fire soon.' He walked toward a bucket near the fire, took out a stick topped with a bundle of petrol-soaked rags, and moved toward the bonfire. All of those present had been waiting for this moment, talking in groups, but always with a wary eye on Dave Corbett, and his flaming brand. There was a hush as he took out his lighter and set the torch flaring into the air. A small cheer went up as he held the torch aloft, advancing on the bonfire with deliberately slow steps.

'Get on with en, Davey bwoy,' a voice called from the crowd, and a small laugh rippled around. We all knew Dave was milking the moment, though none begrudged him.

He gave the torch a final flourish and plunged it into the base of the bonfire. For a few moments the fire played around the flaming torch, its light diffused by sticks and remnants of plant boxes. Then it flared, crackling up into the centre of the towering heap, with a ferocity that suggested a great deal of 'magic fire water' in its depths.

A cheer rang out, louder than before as Dave ran off to the boards and buckets where his 'set' pieces were erected. He lit one and stumbled back a few paces as a rocket shot into the sky. The crowd cheered even louder, and settled into laughter as Dave leaped from one piece to the next, aided and abetted by his daughters who ran to and from the lidded box for smaller items contributed by the visitors.

Then the guy joined in as a series of small detonations made the burning effigy jerk and twitch like a body riddled with machine-gun fire. A Sayers Common guy that wasn't stuffed with crow-scarers would hardly have been a guy at all. Still it crashed, and banged and gyrated.

Then noise was all around me. A vast explosion from behind the melee.

I found myself almost lifted from my feet and half dragged toward the house a few hundred yards away. People all around were fleeing in the same direction like cattle from a blow-fly. I twisted my head round to look behind, and saw a mass of coloured fire emerging from a point to the left of the bonfire. My father parked me next to my mother and raced back toward the conflagration.

I stood watching, a little afraid, until I gradually made sense of the exodus. The firework chest was emitting a mass of sparks and noise. Men were stringing out into a line to pass buckets toward the conflagration. Always the fire precautions were there, but never before had they been needed. People stood in huddles; curiously quiet now that they were not immediately near the noise and heat. In a few minutes it was over. Just the bonfire burned, a crow-scarer exploding every half minute, louder than they had first seemed now in an eerie quiet.

'Everyone all right?' My father asked when he finally trudged back to us.

'Yes. Thank God,' Mother replied.

'Len?'

She waved a hand toward a gaggle of lads collecting at the far side of the yard. 'He's back there. He's okay. What happened?'

Father spread his hands. 'Who can say? A flame, a spark? Something set the firework chest alight.'

'Anyone hurt?' She asked, anxious suddenly.

'Only Steve Garton,' he replied. 'Burned his hand and his eyebrows. Not serious I don't think.'

'Oh?'

'Well, we can't point fingers, but…'

'Hope it hurts him. Little sod needs teaching a lesson. He's little bloody tearaway. I feel sorry for Babs. She didn't deserve those two. No one would. She's got enough on her plate with her Arthur being struck down.'

'Yeah,' Father put a hand on her arm. 'Not now Marg. Please?'

I frowned. 'Is that all the fireworks?' I asked. 'What about my rockets?'

'All gone,' He said. 'They were all in the box.'

'Oh,' I glowered toward the spot were the chest had been. 'You wait till I see those Garton boys. I'll give en what for.' I started toward the fire.

Father grabbed me by the arm. 'You can't see en now. His uncle's taking him to hospital.'

'Don't care,' I snapped. 'I'm gonna get 'im. That liddle bagger owes me three and nine pence.'

'Language,' Mother said, and then looked away, as did my father. As they walked toward the house I heard my father say, 'Poor Stevie. Hospital and our Suzy on the warpath. Life's gonna be 'ard fer that lad fer a while.'

'That's his own fault, 'Mother replied. 'It'll learn him.'

I frowned again. Was my mother really laughing?

*

Wally ambled into the yard far earlier than usual the following morning. He paused, and eased a tobacco tin from his pocket with a conspiratorial air, unhurried, despite the fine drizzle that had just begun to fall. He looked at my father for a long quiet moment, a twinkle around his eyes. He was bursting with something; even I could see that. I slowed my scooping of sheep-feed into a hessian sack, to listen in.

'Had a bit of excitement las' night then,' Wally said. 'Them old Garton bwoys did 'ave a bit of fun I 'erd.'

'You might say,' my father replied. 'Hard to say if was meant of not. I doubt they intended any harm. They just 'aven't got a full deck between them.'

'Arr,' Wally agreed, nodding slowly. 'They'm always bin a bit okkerd. Led their poor old mother a right dance since they could walk.' He laughed, a rusty, hissing sound, like leaking bellows. 'Bugger, bwoy. They'll met their end a lot sooner'n they think, them two will. I c'uld open a book on en.'

'You wouldn't get many takers Wal. I think most people would agree with you.'

'Arr,' he nodded again.

'You didn't make it up the common yourself then? I thought you and Alby liked a glass or two. Old Corbett has a good barrel going in his shed.

'We would, as a rule.' Wally went on teasing tobacco strands in and out of the tin. My father and I waited. His fidgeting tobacco was a sure sign of more to come.

'Yer,' Wally mumbled, finally. 'That's another thing. Don't you go givin' moi old Dad no more o' that they parz'mut wine.'

'Why not?' Father looked guilty. 'Didn't make him ill did it?'

Wally paused in his careful sorting of the dark brown, aromatic tobacco and picking out a half used packet of green Rizla papers. He stuck one paper to his lower lip ready to make his 'roll-up'. He nodded slowly at his own thoughts. Tiny rainwater pear-drops gathered at the edge of his cloth cap, water resistant from greases collected over years of labouring. The droplets flickered on the rim as he moved his head, scattering in small showers of their own. 'Arr,' he muttered to himself.

Like his father, Alby, Wally seldom completed sentences, preferring to listen, adding the odd, 'Arr, Arr,' or a stronger, 'booger Arr!' when occasion demanded. Only tone and inflection changed in this near-wordless communication.

I watched him prepare the cigarette, holding my breath for fear of dislodging the Rizla if I exhaled too hard. The oblong of paper flapped, as he muttered. I was mesmerised, certain it would fly away like a small white butterfly.

'Wahl,' Wally drawled, finally, 'I don't know about ill bwoy, but when I got 'ome the cart was out in the yard, shafts up, with mangolds all over the shop, an' that greedy old baggin' 'oss was out loose, wi' all 'er harness still on', 'elpin of 'erself.' Wally peeled the paper from his lip and trickled a meagre line of tobacco along its length, rolling it into an impossibly thin cigarette, licked and stuck it so his satisfaction, before he began to flick repeatedly at an ancient Zippo lighter. 'Oi shouted up the old'n,' he mumbled between flicks, 'but oi didn' get no answer. He wern't in th'ouse, and I see there wus still chik'ns to get fed, and no tea out, no nuthin'. So I goes back out to th' yard, and caught up old Doll, and oi wus shovin' 'er in the stall, when I 'erd this noise.' The lighter flared suddenly, covering the lid in blue and yellow flame, and Wally, unperturbed by the conflagration, tilted his head to light up, whilst flames licked at his cap. Satisfied at last he slid the Zippo into his pocket.

We waited patiently as Wally closed his eyes against the smoke and drew on the cigarette. It glowed rich orange for two seconds; and promptly went out. 'Wahl,' he said, fishing for the Zippo, 'Oi looks round the tack stall, and there wuz moi old Dad, sat in the feed bin with an' old calf-powder sack over 'is fizzog, snorin' 'is baggin' 'ed orf.' He grinned suddenly, shoulders heaving with a silent laugh as he lit up once more. 'We'am still got mangolds all over th' yard, but they c'n stay there for a bit. They b'aint doin' no 'arm. That old sod put en there. Ee c'n baggin well shovel 'em up fer hisself when ee do feel loike it.'

Parsnip Wine

5 lb parsnips

2 lb loafsugar

1 grapefruit

½ oz fresh yeast

Slice of toast

Method

1. Peel and slice the parsnips; they should now weigh four pounds.

2. Put into a pan with the water and boil until the parsnips are very soft.

3. Strain through muslin and squeeze to extract all of the liquid.

4. Add sugar and juice of the grapefruit. Boil for 45 mins.

5. Pour into a crock.

6. When parsnip liquid is lukewarm spread yeast onto the toast and float it on the top.

7. Cover and leave, stir gently every day for 14 days.

8. Strain and ferment in a jar with an airlock.

9. When fermentation is complete bottle and store for a minimum of six months.

10. As with all root crop wines parsnip wine can be very strong, so beware. It also improves with keeping, so try to leave it for at least one year, preferably two.

11. Most root crops can be made into wine – the exceptions to my knowledge being potatoes and turnips. If you aren't sure about properties of a particular vegetable – *don't use it.*

Mangold Wurzel Wine

4 lb mangolds (mangold wurzels)

3 lb demerara sugar

1 gall water

A few hops are optional and/or according to taste.

Method

1. Clean and slice the mangolds (do not use the crowns)
2. Boil the slices in the water with the hops for two hours.
3. Put the sugar into a crock and pour over the strained mangold liquid.
4. Stir until all of the sugar is dissolved.
5. Set with yeast and leave for a few days.
6. Strain into a fermentation jar with a lock.
7. When fermentation has finished bottle the wine and store for six months before drinking.

Medicinal – Parsnips

Parsnips do not seem to have much history with healers, though it is said they may have some power to aid the cure of snake bites.

They are said to help shift wind.

Traditional – Parsnips

Country folk will tell you that parsnips are sweeter after 'frosting' and crops are often left in the ground until after the first frosts of winter. This stands for kitchen use as well as wine making.

It is said that parsnip seeds should be sown whilst 'still eating the Christmas bread'.

Also the parsnip's notorious slow rate of germination is attributed to the seedling 'going three times to the devil' before it appears above ground. (Though if you sow almost any seed in December I doubt it would germinate *too* rapidly.)

Medicinal/Traditional – Mangold Wurzel

Few references, either medicinal/folklore.

Its main purpose seemed to be as a winter feed for livestock.

It was used for Halloween (or bonfire night) celebrations as carved out candle lanterns before the larger, and more easily excavated, Pumpkin took over. These hollowed out lanterns were called Punkies, and would be carried in procession from door to door with the chant of 'give us a candle, give us a light.' From personal experience I can say that though they were harder to hollow out they lasted longer, and smelled less offensive when they had been carved for a day or two.

Turnips and swedes were often used for the same purpose – though mangolds were considered better. The carved patterns could be of dragons, flowers, stars, crescent moons, etc. Sadly modern affectations have seen the jack o'lantern take an almost exclusive hold on Punkie style.

More modern times have seen the *wurzel* take on its own persona with the popular children's stories of Wurzel Gummidge – which are magical tales with obvious roots in ancient folklore with the Crow-man, et al.

Cider a'Wassail

'Tis the last one,' said Wally. 'An' not too soon, neither. I reck'n we'll be havin' some hard frost later on.' He picked up both his swop and bill hooks, and whetting rod, and dropped them into the sackcloth bag that all of the labourers manufactured for their work tools. 'We c'n get the salvage cleared when we lays this lot come the lambin's over

'I think you're right. It'll sweeten the parzmuts anyway.' My father jammed the final wattle fence panel into the gap in the hawthorn hedge that they had been working on and gave the top a satisfied pat for a job well done.

'Reck'n,' Wally said. 'Don't know about you, bwoy, but I'm goin' 'ome. I'm fair shrammed in this wind. And young maid there's near on starved o' cold.'

I grinned at them, but carried on raking twigs. The ground was frost-hardened and made the going hard on welly-booted feet, and I had long since lost contact with my toes. Even my chilblains were too numb to itch. The only way to remain anything vaguely resembling warm was to keep moving.

The smell of wood smoke wafted all around us and across the fields on a biting wind. The column of white smoke grew thicker and darker, billowing outwards, as I forked another mass of cuttings onto the bonfire. The moisture of both sap and frozen dew fizzed and hissed, adding steam to the mass. I waited for a moment, until I was sure that the addition would burn, before returning to the task of raking more clippings from the frith that my father and Wally had been cutting from the hedgerow.

From the start of lambing to end of harvest they seldom had time for hedging and ditching, but this stretch bordered the lambing pastures, and my father could not afford for his ewes to wander off for seclusion to give birth, as was their habit. Over the autumn and winter ramblers and fishermen had forced passage through the hedges and created unmissable opportunities for the habitual escapees of the farm's small flock of Southdown/Suffolk crosses. An afternoon's work had seen a half dozen wattle fence panels laced into the biggest holes until the hedge could be properly 'laid'. 'That should hold it,' he said. 'We can clear up and take a last check round the lambers before we go in for dinner.' He ruffled my hair as he passed. 'You're doing a grand job, poppet. I'll give you an orange for Christmas.'

'Bain't Christmas,' I replied.

'Ah, then you'll have to wait a bit then, won't you?'

'You've got some pears back 'ome, still.'

My father paused, drawing breath in mock horror. 'Pears? You mean those Williams your mum bought me for special?'

I nodded.

'But I've only got two left.'

'I'll share one with you for puddin'.'

'You drive a hard bargain,' he rubbed at his chin, pretending to think about it. 'All right. Half.'

I grinned, and stuck the pitchfork into another heap of clippings. Wages negotiated I was happy to finish the task, and happier still to have turned one of my father's well-worn sayings back on itself. I could only tweak that one just before and after Christmas, as we seldom had oranges at any other time of the year. Not that I liked them much anyway, I preferred bananas, but they were as Father would have said, as rare as hen's teeth in the Birch household.

'That's it then. No more on, let it die back.' My father kicked some straggles of wood into the fire's embers and took a careful look along the row they had just mended. 'All done.' He grabbed up his own billhook and placed it carefully into his sackcloth bag along with stone, swop-hook and stick. He strung the bag's strap over his shoulder and picked up the wooden rake, leaving me to carry the long handled pitchfork.

We paused at the gate to watch the grazing sheep.

'Arr. There's a few looks loike they'll be dropping roight

early,' Wally observed. 'You goin' to get be able t' get orf an' go a'wassail tonight, bwoy?'

'Don't see why not. What time are you starting off?'

'We should be down by the King's 'Ead about foive. Then we goes athirt o'er Box Farm, we'll dup down Spy Lane to the Mill and back up to the Common for old Corbett's place. We'm ending out the Cricketers

'Alby coming this year?'

Wally shrugged, reaching for his baccy tin. 'He dussn't know. Ee's got the screws bad this last fartnit. Ee c'n hardly walk the length of our yard. Roight hatchety with it an' all, ee is.'

'You could hitch up your Dolly,' my father said, grinning. 'We could all have a lift. We might even get round Withy Farm and up to my bit. I got a lot o' trees round the back, you know.'

Wally licked and stuck the paper and rammed the roll-up between his lips, puffing hard from the exertion as he lit it and screwed his eyes up against the smoke. 'Whal. You might 'ave an idea there. If'n we puts the bigger cart on. Throw in a few bales fer en to set on. We could get most o'the bwoys on board.'

'And the rest can ride their bikes?' My father said.

Wally took a long drag and laughed slowly, a wheezing trickle of faint sound. 'Now then. That'd be a sight. Arr. 'Specially ar'ter they'm 'ad a few jugs.'

'Can I come?' I demanded. 'Can I drive Dolly?'

My father shook his head. 'I don't know, Pet. It gets very late you know.'

'Yeah, but Linda's going. She's going with her dad and her gran.'

My father glanced at Wally, who nodded. 'Arr. Wassail captains, don't matter who tis, they dassn't go wassail without Mistress Goody Hurst. Not if they knows what's what.'

'No? Why's that then?'

Wally puffed out his cheeks and pushed his cap back on

his head. 'She's Mistress Hurst,' he replied, finally. 'She'll be there. Anyway,' he gave my father a curiously awkward glance. 'Me'n Barry's goin' ferret'n s'arteroon. Tekin' a look down the warren by Hope's Gore.'

I wondered, briefly, why the subject was always changed so abruptly but dismissed it as another adult oddity. Goody Hurst seemed to have that effect on quite a few of the village people. I always found her a wonderful old lady. As round as she was high, and as jolly as plump ladies were supposed to be; but who, in my experience, often weren't. She made sweets and fruit drinks for any children who strolled into her tiny cottage, and grew more flowers in her sprawling garden than anyone else that I knew. Most gardens belonging to her friends' families were taken up with veg and fruit to augment the family diet. Growing flowers was a luxury, unless they were marigolds and suchlike that dissuaded garden pests.

'Just the three of us?' My father was asking.

'Whal. Alby might be up to a liddle walk. Do 'im good. And Eddy says ee's got a new jill he wants to try out.'

'If it goes to ground I'm not digging,' My father said quickly. 'Not when the grounds this 'ard.'

'Nor me. Bugger, bwoy. You'll need a 'lectric shovel to get down a warren this weather.'

My father laughed and pushed away from the gate. 'I'll give it a couple o' hours. See you around two?'

'Arr.' Wally ambled off to pick his bike from the hedge close to the gate.

'Can I come ferret'n?' I asked 'Can I, Dad?'

'If your mum says so. You sure you're not cold?'

'Not that cold,' I replied. 'Just my feet. I'll put on another pair of socks.'

'We'll see,' he replied.

I sighed. We'll see was usually a way of not saying no until it was too late.

'You c'n 'ave my pear.' I grabbed Dad's arm and hugged it. 'All en it.'

'Oh … if your mum says yes. All right?'

'Now there's a maid uz knows 'ow to get round 'er old man. Top brick orf the chimberley, I reck'n.'

My father flushed, and grinned. 'She's not been well. She could do with a treat or two.'

'Arr. That's true enough. Anyways, I'm orf. See you s'arternoon.'

'Right'o Wally.' My father raised a hand briefly in salute as Wally pedalled a sedate way homewards.

*

As luck would have it my mother was going shopping that afternoon, her monthly trip into Guildford, and was happy not to have a child in tow demanding things she could not afford to buy. As Len was out doing his 'Saturday' job as van boy helping the Stores with their bread rounds, I would be all alone in the house; and though I was almost in my teens mother still didn't like leaving me alone for too long. So, donning the promised extra socks, and grabbing emergency rations of a half packet of Rich Tea from the larder and a small flask of tea, I cycled down to Hope's Gore with my father. Across my back a bag of purse nets bumped and swayed precariously. My father tied a small shovel to his crossbar and tucked the canvas bag containing his ferrets inside his jacket to shield them from cold.

'You won't arf cop it off Mum, putting ferrets in your coat,' I told him. 'It'll stink something rotten.'

'Don't tell her, then.'

'Won't af'to. That coat'll walk in the house on its own.'

'Don't you worry, pet. Your mum's bark is a lot worse than the bite.'

'Yeah.' I was non-committal. In my experience Mother's bark and bite were a perfect match. She prided herself on 'never making a threat she wouldn't carry out'. This mostly came in the form of the disciplinary rule of three. Tell 'em, warn 'em, wallop 'em. I tried hard not to fall foul of either one.

As we neared the copse that bordered one side of the Gore I saw a gaggle of men sheltering from the wind among the trees. Wally and Alby I knew, and also Jimmy Shotter and Wally's cousin, Barry. With them was a youth who looked vaguely familiar, but whom I was fairly certain I had never come across before.

My father coasted to a halt and propped his bike among the rest that were laced in a tangle of pedals and handlebars around a small oak tree. 'Are we fit, then?' he asked.

'Reck'n,' Alby replied through his roll-up. 'You knows' Eddy, don't you, bwoy?'

'Eddy Joyce?'

'Arr.'

'I've heard. Afternoon Eddy.'

'Mr Birch,' the lad mumbled.

'Your mum any better?'

Eddy scowled and shook his head, his face tingeing pink. 'Nope,' he muttered.

I stared at him, hard. So this was Eddy. Like my father, I had heard of him, brother to the hapless Bob and cousin to Linda; and, according to whom, a lad who was only marginally more able than his sibling. Knowing what a pack of teasers these men could be I felt we could look forward to a little excitement. I left my bike with the rest of the stack and followed the group across the rough grass of the gore toward the bank on the far side where there was known to be a huge warren.

'Are we long netting today?' My father asked.

'Not enough time,' Wally replied. 'Not if we wants to get out later on.'

'Fair enough. I brought some small nets.'

'Good on'yer. Let's 'ave'm then. Bwoy.'

The process began by pegging a purse net over all of the bolt-holes, and weighting them with stones. I was relegated to standing back and watching over the sacks of ferrets. Five canvas bags, each tied at the neck with string and each one writhing and turning, emitting small squeaks and grunts as the occupants alternately played and fought each other, and sought a way out. Like their water-born brother-otter, ferrets are great comedians whose life is spent eating, sleeping and playing, though not necessarily in that order. I loved to watch Fifi and Freda when my father let them out of their cage to play. It amused me to watch them bounding across the grass, backs arched, making play lunges at each other and bouncing as high as they could like cream coloured, hairy jumping-jacks.

Standing guard, however, consisted mainly of retrieving any sack that rolled away from the pile, and tapping lightly with a short stick when the sounds of a less than happy scrap became too obvious.

In a very short space of time the holes had been stopped, and only a few major entrances remained. The men returned to the sacks and paused for a well earned *roll-up*.

Barry pulled a harness from his pocket, from which hung a tiny bell. 'If'n its all roight with you lot. I'm bellin'. There's too many roots along this way fer lines.'

'Me an' all,' Wally drawled. 'Stan bain't got no problem with his two. Gurt big maids e's got, an' fast too. What about you Eddy? You got your uncle Sid's old jill?'

Eddy shook his head. 'No,' he declared, his chest puffing visibly. 'I got my own. Tis a nice liddle hob off his jill's last brood.'

There was a short silence. I could see a few faces struggling to hide smiles and I could see why. Hobs were notoriously lazier than their female counterparts, and unless they were especially hungry, much preferred chasing a jill to rabbits, or failing that curling up and going to sleep. Even I knew that much. Some people did hunt with hobs, but jills were the gender of choice.

'Oh arr?' said Wally. ''Ave en been out with it before?'

'No.'

'Roight then,' he relit his cigarette and bent to lift the sack containing his own prized jill and opening the neck to release her. The jill slithered around his neck and nuzzled at the back of his cap, before nosing into the harness that Wally held ready for her. As he buckled it on the bell chinked shrilly in the crisp air. 'Best let the ladies go in fust orf. And then you can give your little lad a try. Seein as e's just larnin'.'

Eddy hesitated, but then nodded; lowering the sack he had just lifted back to the ground once more.

The men advanced on the warren. Wally set his animal down first and she slid into the burrow eagerly, the bell tinkling for only a very short time before she was out of sight. It was just a few minutes before the first rabbit shot from a hole a few yards away, struggling frantically in the folds of the purse. Wally was onto it, giving the animal a sharp clout with his short stick 'Good start,' he held up a plump corpse and then bent to re fix the net.

Within the space of a few minutes a half dozen rabbits had bolted into the nets before the jill appeared in hot pursuit. Wally snatched her up and fondled her, then, tucking her into is jacket, he rapidly paunched a carcass and offered her a small chunk of the liver as a reward. He settled her back into her sack and took up his station as Barry and Jimmy let their animals in together for their turn. After them it was Fifi and Freda's turn and between them my father's girls routed another five rabbits.

'Not a bad bag,' said my father. 'You gonna give your boy a chance now, Ed?'

'Put a line in en,' said Jimmy. 'Fust time out you don't want 'im to go missin.'

Ed nodded and tied a long ball of twine to his hob's harness. He let him go, playing out several yards of string before it went slack. He frowned, and tugged on the line. They all waited. Minutes ticked by.

'Gorn to ground,' Wally said. 'Better start diggin', bwoy.'

He threw Eddy a shovel and sat on a fallen tree to smoke in comfort. 'Want a suck?' He waved a small bottle of rum and then tossed it gently to my father.

He took it, uncorked and took a small swallow. 'Keeps the cold out,' he said and took a place on the log next to Wally. Before long all of them were sitting on the fallen tree, sipping rum and paunching their catch, and egging Eddy on with 'helpful' hints as he began to dig.

I ran back to my bike for the flask. I would have liked to have tasted the rum, but I knew my father would never allow it. He allowed me a sup at his homemade wine, but never spirits.

The ground was hard-packed, even though it was sandy and well tilled from centuries of rabbit occupation. It was almost an hour before Ed turned up his errant hunter, curled asleep with the remains of a young rabbit that he had run to ground

The men began to laugh.

'Well, ee caught it any how,' said Barry.

'But ee's kippin on the job,' Jimmy added.

'You know what, bwoy?' Alby slapped Ed on the shoulder. 'Ee wants a bigger bloody bell. Keep en awake'.

Ed swore, and snatched up the animal angrily, and then howled in pain. Equally angry having been snatched from his meal, the hob had turned on its own length and sunk his yellow teeth into Eddy's finger.

Partly because of its dentistry, and in some part through its cussed nature, once a ferret bites it is notoriously hard to dislodge. Eddy shook his hand, attempting to rattle it loose. It hung from his finger, squeaking angrily, blinking its eyes and flailing its limbs, but refusing to drop off.

The men grouped around the boy, happy to poke fun, but not wanting either boy or beast to be hurt badly.

'Blow on en,' Alby said.

'What?' Eddy sobbed.

'In ens face,' Barry said. 'Blow, and he'll let go.'

Eddy glanced around him warily. I could see he only half believed them. 'Blow?' he said.

'Arr,' said Wally. 'Blow 'ard.'.

Eddy drew breath and blew a long stream of air, which turned to mist in the cold.

The ferret did let go, just for a moment, blinking, agitated by this new assault on its person, then seeing where the breeze was coming from, retaliated; fastening onto Eddy's bottom lip in an eye's wink.

Ed screamed.

I was amazed the hob didn't let go when that blast of noise rushed past its ears, but it hung on tight.

'You daft liddle bugger,' Alby snapped. 'Short blows, not a bloody 'urricane.' He reached for the hob and took its weight to stop it tearing the lad's lip any further.

'Blow,' Jimmy shouted, between guffaws.

Eddy tried, huffing short breaths between sobs. Blood streamed from his mouth splashing both his jacket and the hob in a red shower.

I watched, fascinated. It was funny, in a macabre fashion, though slightly nauseating at the same time.

Alby shouted at Eddy to 'Stand fast, you juggeren yaffler.' He waited until Eddy had stopped jigging from foot to foot before he blew a short blast at the animal's face, jerking his head back to avoid the same fate as the hob's young master.

The ferret released the lip and looked around, his head whipping to and fro in sharp, jagged moves.

'Fuss en,' Wally said. 'Goo on Ed. Ee's afrit. Ee won't ever be no good if you don't tame 'im proper.'

'I'll wring 'is bloody neck,' Ed snapped, dabbing at his mouth with his sleeve.

'Ee's yorn,' said Barry. 'Tame 'im up.'

'Don't wan 'im. 'Orrible thing,' Ed wailed. 'Ee 'urt me.'

'Ahhh, Poor puddin',' said Wally, dripping derision. 'Better run on 'ome to yer gran'n get that mouth sewed up.' He swept the hob from Alby and shoved it back into its bag.

'I'll have the varment for you. Let me know if'n you wants en back.'

Ed ran across the grass, grabbed his bike and was gone.

'Will he be all right?' My father asked. 'That was a nasty bite.'

'Ee'll be orl' roight.' Alby replied. 'Twas just a biddy suck his old hob give en. Not so sure about his old gran, though. I reck'n she'll take 'er ladle to 'im fer bein' so daft.' He shook his head. 'They're both a bit slow, those boys. Their old man was a ha'penny short. Shame, but there you are. God put them 'ere. They must 'av a purpose.'

'Arr,' said Wally. 'To give us a good larf.'

*

'You comin' wassailing with us, Len?'

My brother looked up and sneered. 'Singing to trees?' He shook his head. 'It's daft.'

'I'm not sure our Suzie aught to be going either,' my mother added. 'It's getting very cold out there.'

'I'll be all right, Mum. Linda's goin'. So's Jackie, and Goody Hurst, and lots of people. Pleeeese, Mum.' I grabbed my mother's hand and gazed up at her. 'I won't get too cold, honest. I'll wear two vests. And Goody Hurst says, I can stay at hers if it gets late. Pleeeeeese, Mum. Can I?'

Mother shook her head, and smiled one of her rare smiles. 'Two vests? Any other time it's World War Three getting you to wear one.' She glanced at my father and shook her head again. 'All right. But try not to keep her out too late, Stan, love. She shouldn't get cold air on her chest. You know what Doctor Kelsey said.'

'She'll be fine. We don't go right up to the village, only the common. The village's got its own team. Or they did have. Alby said they might not have enough for a proper round this year.' He shrugged, dismissing the doings of the villagers in an instant. 'Any way, if Goody Hurst changes her mind we'll be swinging this way near the end, so she can come home then if she's not warm enough.'

Mother nodded, mollified for the moment, and looked at me, sternly. 'Wear your woolly tights under your trousers, and your ear-flap hat.'

I nodded. I hated that hat with a passion, it made my ears itch, but I could make the sacrifice in a good cause. And I had no intention of missing the party that Linda assured me would happen when the singing was over.

The afternoon light was fading as we set off, and I had managed to get away with just the one vest. I pedalled furiously behind my father, the dynamos humming loudly, and still the lamps produced only pale glimmers of dullest light before us.

By the time we reached the end of the lane, and stacked the bikes in the copse, Wally and Alby were already waiting on the roadway. Dolly, lightly rugged against the cold, was huffing and fidgeting, shaking her head and chewing at her bit in disgust. She was unused to nocturnal ramblings, especially in this sort of weather, and made her feelings clear.

I paused to pluck a handful of frosty grass stems and proffered them to the horse as a peace offering. Dolly took them, mumbled them around her mouth for a few moments and let them drop. Crestfallen, I went to climb into the back of the cart.

'Don't you mind 'er, maid,' Alby laughed. 'She's all of a flim-flam, comin' out when she reck'ns she aught'a be asleep.' He flicked the reins gently. 'Got the 'ump, b'aint en old Gurrl?'

Dolly flicked her ears back to take in the tone of her master's comment and pulled at the bit before deciding that she would, after all, move on, Wally walking at her side with a lantern to guide us in the dark.

We stopped to pick up a few more people along the common before reaching Goody Hurst's cottage, just yards from the pub. A small gathering of people stood close to her gate, chatting among themselves. Many wore the blacked faces and ragged cloaks, and carried the stout sticks and drums, of the Morris-men. Though not all, I noted, were actually men.

Dolly slowed to a halt, snuffling at the bit, and rumbling quietly to herself; obviously still put out by this late outing. When she halted a cheer went up, and as if by a signal the 'dancers' parted into two lines, their sticks touching across the path. The cottage door opened with a flourish, and Goody Hurst appeared, clad all in black, from her freshly cleaned wellies up to a long large felt hat rammed around her ears. The hat was decorated with the same strips of rag and tethers of ivy that bedecked the dancers' cloaks. She held aloft a large wooden bowl hung with red, green and white ribbons, and strands of fresh greenery.

The musicians began a quiet dance song, a tune that was both merry and curiously solemn at the same time. Goody Hurst walked sedately down her path, between the arched arms of her baton-wielding escort, followed by her unusually-demure granddaughters, Linda and Jackie. The songs of drum, fiddle and whistle padded softly around her through the dusk.

My father placed a restraining hand on my shoulder, but I needed no such warning as to how solemn the occasion was. It felt like a school assembly or perhaps closer to a church service when the demeanour of everyone around was so respectful; even awestruck. I tried to catch Linda's eye, but my friend stared pointedly ahead as Goody Hurst reached the cart and handed the decorated bowl to Alby, who, to my amazement, bowed low as he received it. The moment lingered holding back time for a breath or two, but as the music struck a jauntier note, it was washed away. Tension dissipated, Goody Hurst hauled herself onto the cart, amid her customary banter with the slyly witty Charmans.

I knew that Alby was Wassail Captain, and had been for some years, but even I could not miss drawing the obvious conclusion of who was actually in charge of proceedings.

Goody Hurst took her seat at the head of the cart, on a throne of hay bales with Linda and Jackie near her feet, their parents walking beside the cart.

'You got 'ere, then?' said Linda. She leaned over and handed me a spice cake. 'I thought your old mum might've said no.'

I took the proffered cake eagerly. 'She was shopping today. Put her in a good mood I think. An' she says yes I c'n stay at your Gran's if it gets late.'

'It will,' Linda assured me. Gran said we're doin' a couple've extras tonight, if we can, cos the villagers aren't out this year.'

'Which ones?'

'Dunno.'

I glanced around me. 'Not as many here as I thought there'd be.'

'Never is.' Linda replied.

'And then they'll wonder why they need all this poison stuff to grow apples,' Goody Hurst observed.

I looked at Linda, who lowered her eyes, embarrassed. I wondered what had been meant by that cryptic comment, but it was fairly obvious I wasn't going to get any clarification. I turned my attention to the singing that had broken out among those walking by the cart. Songs that I had often heard in harvest suppers, and even, at times, in the fields; like *Sussex Ploughboy, Shepherd of the Downs* and *John Barleycorn*. Plus a few more seasonal ones that I did not hear at school or church; *The Echoing Horn* and *The Mistletoe Bough*.

The few other children and elderly folk present were given seats on the cart, and the procession moved off toward the first port of call, Box Farm. As we drew up to the farmhouse door, we began singing the traditional round.

Here we come a 'wassailing
Among the leaves so green
Here we come a 'dancing

So fair to be seen
Love and joy unto you
And for you a wassail too
Goddess bless you
And send you a happy new year
Goddess send you a happy new year.

By the time the round had finished we were all dismounted and gathered on the path, waiting in a noisy huddle while Alby and Wally filled the bowl from a small keg of cider that the resident farmer, Sid Grinstead brought from the house. Alby, followed by Goody Hurst, and the rest of the group walked down to the orchard.

Some one began '*The Husbandman*', and by the time they reached the orchard wall the chorus was swelling into the cold night air, and making my neck prickle. I glanced at Linda and grinned.

Alby Charman and Goody Hurst walked the bowl to the largest (and oldest) tree, and stopped. Goody Hurst took out a small bowl and lobbed chunks of toast into whilst Alby ladled cider over the top. The band struck up a dance tune and the dancers danced, while Alby and Goody Hurst stuck cider-soaked toast into the forks of the branches. Then, at some signal that I didn't see they all stopped.

'For the Robin,' Goody Hurst called.

Alby stepped forward and ladled cider around the roots of the tree, whilst everyone present circled it, banging drums and chanting.

Here stands a jolly good old apple tree
Stand fast, root; bear well, top
Every little bough,
Bear an apple now;
Every little twig,
Bear an apple big;
Hats full, caps full!

Whoop whoop holloa!
Blow, blow the horn
Fire the gun!
Spirits be gone!

We all bellowed the second verse, banging an assortment of pots and lids, whilst Wally fired his old shot gun through the branches. Then we ended with a huge, roaring cheer that bubbled into excited laughter and chatter as we trooped back to the house for spice biscuits, honey cakes and mugs of mulled cider.

'Mrs Hurst,' I said, as we stood in the yard, sipping at the hot liquid. 'Why give robins soggy toast?'

Goody Hurst laughed, quietly. 'Cos ee's an old one, my pet. Older'n me, even.' She tilted her head to peer at me, almost robin like, herself at that moment. ''Tis an old habit. The Robin's like another name for the tree-spirits. Them's Fairieses.'

'Now, Ma,' George said, sidling up to his mother from behind the cart. 'Don't you go fillin' these maid's heads with your old nonsense. Stan's missus, she's a chapel goin' woman. She won't thank en.'

''Tis nothing these maids shouldn't hear,' she replied, sharp toned, her eyes flashing. 'An' nothin' you bain't bin told a 'undred times.'

'Arr,' he agreed. 'But that's me.' He winked and withdrew into the shadows once more.

I wanted to ask Goody Hurst what she meant by spirits, but the old woman had moved on, leaving me with Linda to ponder on the more inscrutable nuances of the adult world.

'Gran and Dad are always 'avin' rows over that one,' Linda observed. 'He don't think Gran should be passing on all she knows to me'n Jackie.'

'And what do you know?' I asked.

'Not a lot,' Linda admitted, pulling a face. 'Gran says I'm too young yet, but she'll teach me when I'm our Jack's age.'

I sighed, and patted my friend's arm. 'I know how you feel. Taint fair, being the youngest, is it?' I put my mug on the churn-pier and jumped back into the cart. 'Come on, Linda. We'll be off, d'rectly.'

The procession moved on, stopping at the Mill and Cobbett's Nursery as planned, plus Avons Farm and the Manor, and even sweeping through the small orchard at Withy Farm. By this time it was getting late, and the dancers and followers distinctly unsteady. Imbibing cider at every stop was taking its toll. Even we girls, who had been given ginger pop after the first sip of cider, were feeling worse for wear.

We drew up at Goody Hurst's house at almost ten. The singers and dancers and musicians alike tumbled into her cottage for a well-earned supper. As well as the spice and honey cakes there were potatoes that had been baking in the low oven since our departure, and a cauldron of vegetable soup to warm *shrammed* bones. Pies and bread and cheese lurked beneath a snowy cloth that Goody Hurst flicked from her kitchen table with a flourish.

'Dig in,' she urged us. 'Plenty more to come.'

We grabbed soup and bread and retreated to the parlour, stoking the embers of the fire into life once more before settling into the sunken-seated horsehair couch.

'Whal?' Linda drawled. 'Wuz it good, then?'

I nodded eagerly, chewing quickly to rid myself of a huge chunk of bread. 'Really good,' I said. 'I like all the singin' an' stuff.'

'An' me. Tis a shame there's so many folks don't want to know.'

I shrugged. 'Tis their problem.'

Goody Hurst appeared, followed by a few other of the party goers. 'Twill be yours when you gets older,' Goody Hurst said. 'Not many wassailers left now.'

We sat in silence, eating and drinking; listening sleepily to the buzz of voices, and the odd snatch of song as more of the revellers joined them around the fire. After a while the conversation grew less, and the songs longer. Lilting ballads became the order of the day, pleasantly gentle after the rousing Wassail fare. We wilted against each other, and drifted on the songs toward another morning.

Cider

By its very nature cider making is pretty much one of trial and error; until, that is, experience takes over. There are no exact quantities, or any absolutes in method or timescale.

The apples should be picked ripe and left for a few days to soften a little. Any apples can be used, and a mix of varieties is preferable for domestic use. But if you can get hold of some of the traditional cider apple varieties you will notice a difference.

Using a proportion of windfalls is acceptable, as a few bruised fruits do not affect the finished product, but cider should not be made wholly of damaged fruit. As varieties will vary in juice content a rough guide to quantities is ten to fourteen lbs of apples to make one gallon of cider.

Crush your apples. You can use a food processor, though if you are making any quantity this will take a while. On farms crushing would have been done with a horse-drawn stone wheel turning in a circular stone trough, or else with a cider 'press' in which apples are roughly broken, wrapped with sacking into flat 'cakes' and stacked in the flat bed of the press.

A board attached to a turn screw is placed on the top and wound down until all the liquid has run from the pulp. The juice is collected via runnels at the corners of the bed.

Farmers would use the left over apple-pulp to feed pigs or cattle. You may find you can hire a small press from some wine maker's shops, or from a local wine-making society. If you intend to make cidering an annual affair you could do worse than invest in a press of your own. If you are not good with tools then a carpenter would have no trouble making one for you.

The juice is placed in a barrel and fermented without any further additions (old farm hands will insist that they add a hand of ham or pork, or even insist that no brew is complete without a dead rat or two if they want to add a little shock factor).

The above method will make traditional rough or scrumpy cider. If you prefer sweet cider siphon off the liquid without disturbing the cider dregs and add six pounds sugar to every ten gallons of liquid, and re-ferment.

Sparkling cider can be made by bottling your brew just before the fermentation process has ended.

Test for the right time by taking out half a jar full and leaving it in a warm place for six hours with the lid screwed down.

If it is full of gas and has settled out when you open it leave it for a while longer. It is safe to bottle when it only gives off a little fizz of gas and no sediment is thrown.

Be very careful if you store your cider in screw-top glass vessels after fermentation. If it starts to ferment again you may find yourself host to a rack full of small, but potentially lethal, bombs.

Cider should be kept for at least six months after fermentation has finished.

Note: the above process can also be used with pears to make an acceptable Perry wine.

Medicinal

Cider was sometimes called agricultural brandy, and some old time farm hands will tell you it cures anything and everything; I think it more likely they just didn't notice what they were suffering suffered from after a few pints.

For wine, cider or medicine try to buy organic apples, or better still, grow your own as the chemicals can destroy 'useful' bacteria as well as the harmful.

Raw apples can be used to ease rheumatic pains, colds, intestinal colic, anaemia, constipation, urinary infection and cystitis.

Cooked apple is used for stomach ailments and skin infections, including scabies.

Apple pulp as a facemask will tighten facial tissue.

Rotten apples were applied to toes to cure chilblains

In Sussex it was said that rubbing an apple on a wart would make it drop off.

Traditional

Much of the folklore given to the apple seems to be about finding a partner. For example, peeling an apple in one strip and dropping the peel over your shoulder to form the initial letter of your husband's name – usually done at Halloween.

There are numerous Wassailing traditions up and down the country where apple trees are toasted with libations of their own blood (cider); where sticks are hung from branches; where arrows fired through the trees to drive away evil spirits' or guns; thus guaranteeing a good crop.

In Sussex it is called 'howling' when on Twelfth Night dancers and revellers go to the orchard and make as much noise as possible to scare away the bad spirits. They then give three cheers to the orchard owner and retire to a suitable place to dance, drink cider and eat spices cakes and buns.

Apples hold a great significance in various Pagan beliefs. Cutting an apple across its girth produces a five-pointed star, the Pentagram, and represents the fruitfulness of the Goddess. It is a symbol of Witchcraft. The Apple tree was a holy tree to many cultures.

Getting the Christmas Bird

'It's a one-legged Woozlum.' My father assured me. 'It's a cross between an Oozlum and a Woozle. Very rare.'

I looked down at the row of small round holes that trailed through the snow next to our bootprints and snorted both amusement and exasperation. I loved my fathers' elaborate jokes but there were times when he drove me mad. This one may have worked when I was five but not anymore.

The sledge was heaped high with dark-leaved holly, bundles of ivy, fir swathes and my favourite, the gleaming, orange/pink fruited spindle. I knew they were far more than necessary, but I adored the Christmas ritual of Gathering-the-Greens. It was only I that was really interested, but with my father's help I always made an occasion of it. We had gathered evergreens for swags and left the sledge near the ram's shed before heading toward the Top Close where two-dozen steers were kept on deep litter for the winter months.

It had snowed hard that morning, and the sky promised a lot more to come. Leaden cloud layers spanned the sky and a stiff wind was blowing up from the north.

My father frowned at the sky. I suspect he could have preferred a strapping lad's muscle for this job, but Len had been too engrossed in his model railway to offer. Even the with keenest of intentions my illness kept me small for my age. 'Come on Sunshine,' he said. 'Time we got on. I want to get 'ome to see the football.'

My father moved away, and I had to run to catch up. 'So what's this Oozlum?' I demanded.

'A bird that flies round and round in circles until it disappears...' He paused and coughed loudly. I hid my own smile. I had heard this one a hundred times, yet still he worried that I might go home and repeat the rest of the rhyme to Mother, and then he'd be in trouble. He regrouped and changed tack. 'Related to the Mugwump,' he continued.

I galloped beside my father, laughing, or as near to laughing as I could manage. I was getting out of puff trying to keep up, breath streaming before me in trailing steam-train clouds. The snow was well over my ankles which made the running hard. I scuttled after him, face stinging with the small, gritty snow that had begun to whistle on the tail of the bitter wind.

We paused at the last gate, and I took the brief respite to pursue my interrogation. 'And the Woozlum?' I asked.

My father glanced at me as he pulled the gate toward him with the crook of his walking stick. 'A one legged bird,' he said. 'It hops around the countryside following Heflumps to steal their honey.'

'Oh, Daaad!' I swept up a handful of snow and threw it at him.

My father shook the white powder from his coat, and glanced around him, serious all of a sudden. 'I think we'd better get moving, Pet.' He said. 'That snow's getting thicker. Bo! Come by!'

Bo came bounding through the drifts in a strange rocking-horse stride. His plumed tail whipping and his deep pink tongue lolling.

I threw him a snowball and Bo raced after it, jumped. His jaws snapped and the missile exploded around his head. I shrieked with laughter and bent to gather more snow. The walk became a noisy one as Bo demolished one ball after another, rarely missing his mark.

The Top Barns were almost a mile from the cottage. A collection of barns constructed of pitch-blackened wood and Sussex brick, which had originally been built to house horses. Now they were used to over-winter beef steers, and to store some of the wheat straw from the three-acre field that spread between them and then derelict Arun and Wey canal.

My father opened the small door and we all piled in. Bo crossed straight to the stable door that led to the main barn where the steers were kept. He looked over his shoulder at my father, his tongue still flapping, his sides heaving with spent breath.

'Hang on lad,' my father laughed. He lifted the lid on the two galvanised bins that held opened bags of cow-cake, crushed oats and barley. Supposedly it stopped rodents from eating the feed, but it was a fairly token effort. 'Sheer-meece?' he asked.

It was an old game, one we had played since before I was even tall enough to see over the bin sides and had to stand on a straw bale to play.

I watched avidly as the lid rose, and counted with my fingers as the little furry bodies scampered for cover. Mice of various kinds. The rats were too large to find a way in. 'Seven,' I shrieked. 'I think that's a record'

'Most likely,' my father agreed absently. He bent to scoop feed from the bins into heavy weight sacks, counting under his breath as he did so.

'Shall I do silage?' I asked.

My father shook his head, still counting.

'Hay?'

He nodded.

'How many?' I asked.

'Two,' he said, throwing the scoop into the bin and letting the lid fall with a dull clang. 'Can you roll them down for me? And put en in the barrow?

'Course,' I snorted, and pushed opened the door into the hay store to climb onto the first layer. The barns had no electricity supply, and I had to work from natural light such as it was. The store smelled cool and dusty, and faintly sweet. The barrow stood by the door and I shoved it further into the patch of dim light where I rolled two bales from the stack onto the floor.

I could hear the half-door into the pen opening, and my father's deep voice urging Bo to 'go by, lad'. I hurried to roll one bale through to the doorway. I liked to watch Bo clearing a passage like a furry snowplough.

The steers grunted gently as they pushed and shoved and pushed to get out of the way of the dog's snapping jaws. Bo strutted in front of his master, head and tail held high as he cleaved a path for my father through the forest of stomping legs and barrel-shaped bodies.

Dad stopped by the first of the two centre mangers and poured a steady stream of cattle-feed and corn into the tray, then walked around both mangers, pouring as he went; and behind him the steers fell into rank snuffling and grumbling as they jostled at the manger trays for a share of the feed-stuff. A relative quiet fell over the barn as they all settled, noses down, for their evening feed.

I breathed in deeply, savouring the acrid sweetness of 'cow' mixed with silage from the manger standing at the far end of the barn; where a wagon load of silage was parked on the outside of double doors handy for pitching straight into the mangers.

My father came back to the door and opened it to take the first bale. He lifted it onto a barrow and waited while I rolled up the second bale. Cutting the twine holding the bales tight he wheeled them into the barn, throwing sections of hay into the mangers with a pitchfork.

I breathed in again, smelling the hay and straw, and over them something else that I could not quite place. Not a smell so much as a sensation in my nostrils that could only be the smell of cold that only came with the snow.

I went to the feed room's single dusty window. In the short time that we had been in the hay store the wind's burden of frozen moisture had blossomed into fat, fluttering snow-blobs. 'Blobs,' I decided, 'Far too big for snowflakes.'

'Getting thick,' my father observed as he came to stand beside me. 'Bit of straw to get down,' he said, 'and then we'll go,' he told me. 'Come on Susie giv' us a hand.'

I helped him to take two straw bales to the door, but no further. My father would not let me into the barn, especially when he spread straw because the animals were too boisterous in confined spaces.

He dumped the bales in the centre, cut the twines, took his pitchfork and began shaking the straw across the barn floor, spreading a layer across the dampest patches of deep-litter.

One steer, and then two, and then a whole gang left the mangers and began to rush around in the new straw. My father went on shaking wedges out, Bo standing guard, warning off any steer that came too close as they kicked and bucked and danced through the clean bedding.

I was on the door, my boot toes claiming a hold on the ledge struts. I giggled at the spectacle, as I always did, finding the animal's mood infectious.

'All done,' said my father as he brought back the barrow and fork. 'Time we went before this snow gets worse.'

It took just a few minutes to empty the barrow and check that all the doors were secure before we collected the sledge and began the trek home. Once we had left the lee of the barns the wind hit hard. It was almost a mile from the top-barns to the cottage, and though it was track-way rather than open fields it was hard going. I trudged just behind my father, shielding my face in the folds of my duffel coat hood, my scarf wrapped close around my mouth. Even then some of the snowy lumps found a way into my eyes, melting rapidly as they touched the only exposed part of me. In fact it was hard to see anything beyond my booted feet.

As we came down from the upper fields it got a little less windy, but the snow was falling harder now. The lane cut a dip between the fields, topped on either side by thick hedges that my father and the rest of the farm labourers had spent the autumn layering. Here and there a tall oak or elm tree swayed in the rising wind. Between them some holly trees and bushes rustled their dark spines, left for luck, and covered in bright berries, and it was only these raised bushes and trees that gave any indication of the track's direction.

I found myself beginning to lag behind, and though I tried

to catch up the wind was strong, and the snow dragged at my legs. My father's solid form was only a yard or two away, but was getting hazy in the wind-driven murk of the snowstorm.

One tall holly sentinel dipped toward me flailing its arms. I shied away and tripped, sprawling into the drifting snow. 'Dad,' I yelled. Suddenly I felt five years old and could feel tears prickling among the melted snow. Maybe he wouldn't notice and he would disappear into the whiteness, and then I'd be alone. 'Daddy,' I screamed. 'Daddy, wait, please!'

My father hurried back the few paces between us and handed me his stick. 'I'm sorry, Pet. Here, hang on to this.' Then he pulled me close against him as he turned back into the wind.

I grabbed the stick, panic subsiding immediately. I felt a little foolish. 'My feet are cold,' I said, a sob catching in my throat. 'They're getting fuzzy.'

'Never mind, Pet. We'll be home soon.' My father moved the greenery to the very end of the sledge. 'Good job this thing is built to take three,' he observed. He grasped the stick, leaning on it as he tackled the hill, hauling sledge, daughter and foliage along the final stretch in a silence, made more eerie by the quiet of the snowy landscape.

Bo trotted before us, pausing before the porch door to shake the snow from his thick coat, and jostled through the door as my father pulled it open. He took up the tall metal scuttle that had been left by the kitchen door and filled it before he bent to help me, still struggling with my wellington boots. 'Getting deep,' my father announced as he hustled me across to the Aga to warm myself. 'And ruddy cold.'

'Language,' Mother said absently. 'Are your coats wet?'

My father shook his head. 'It's dry snow. Brushed right off.' He motioned me into the chair by the Aga and bent to rub my feet between his palms. 'Better Cherub?' he asked.

'Yes,' I nodded, grinning now I had warmed up a little.

'Tea will be ready in a bit,' Mother announced. The table was already set with her second best table cloth. Pristine mint green that she had embroidered with anemones and snowdrops; the snow white 'best' cloth was only used for visitors and Christmas Day.

Best cloths meant visitors and I wondered who that could be in this weather, then dismissed the thought and set about weaving the mound of greenery into long bundles.

By six o'clock I had uneven lumpy swags piled on every ledge and picture rail. The ceiling was already a mass of criss-crossing paper chains, manufactured with equal enthusiasm and similar finesse. My parents exchanged glances. There was little they could say without deflating their only daughter's pride.

'It's ... bright,' my father ventured.

'Yes,' I cocked my head from side to side in a serious appraisal. 'But we haven't got the Chinese lanterns up yet. Or those paper-folding-things.'

My father groaned quietly, and Mother returned to the kitchen to finish peeling the vegetables. Their youngest child had far too more energy. 'Overactive,' the specialist had told them. 'Keep her occupied. She'll probably grow out of it.'

Easy said, but harder done, I was eleven, and showed no signs of calming down. That day was all about perfecting decorations.

All Father wanted to do was stretch out in his chair in front of the log fire and watch the News. He knelt down and scooped the wreckage left by my whirlwind activity into the storage box and then turned on the TV. It had been a long afternoon, and he had a four a.m. start for milking the next morning, despite it being Christmas Day.

The TV hummed gently, and the screen's faint greyness lifted to fizzling black and white specks as the valves warmed to life. A face appeared, and then gently vanished off the top of the screen, to be replaced from the bottom. Dad slapped the Bakelite casing and the rolling screen slowed, fuzzing and tweaking to a standstill. A few minutes later Mother appeared with a cup of tea.

'Just watching the news,' he said, guiltily. 'I'll just drink this, and I'll help you out there.'

'Alright,' she did not begrudge him a rest; he worked long hours, and hard ones, as a stockman and labourer, but she resented having so much left to do before she could join him. 'What time's the Guv'nor coming?' she asked.

''Bout eight, he said. 'Plenty of time yet.'

It was the Landlord's habit to visit each employee on Christmas Eve bearing gifts. Sherry for the wife, whisky or rum for the man, biscuits for the children and a turkey from the farms own flock. Mother needed to prepare that bird for cooking and she always said that she'd rather it was stuffed and ready this side of nine o'clock.

Bo whined gently. Like most working dogs he only came in-doors on the coldest of nights, but he sensed the atmosphere was not normal. My father bent to rub the dog's ears briefly.

'Len!' Margery yelled. 'Cocoa!' There came a muffled reply and a thumping of feet as her son pounded into the kitchen.

'I'm starving,' Len announced. 'Got any biscuits, Mum? Please?'

She sighed, but marched into the pantry, to reappear with a tin of Rover Assorted. The annual tin of biscuits was about to be broached. My father took the tin, laboriously peeled of the Sellotape from the rim and prised the lid free. With exaggerated care he removed the paper circle from the top layer, glancing around to make sure that his audience was still attentive. He could never resist teasing.

'Only one,' Mother said sternly.

Len and I pushed forward, scrabbling to beat each other to the chocolate digestives. I hesitated. I loved bourbons the best, but I also liked the pink wafers. On the other hand I looked longingly at the iced shortcake rounds, smooth and shiny in pink, yellow and brown, all decorated with the ghostly white shapes of angels and stars. My left thumb crept into my mouth. My other hand hovered over one biscuit, then another, each morsel snug in its crinkly red-paper nest.

'Can we have another one, Mum?' asked Len. 'It's Christmas,' he added hopefully.

'Oh, all right,' she said, sounding crosser than she was. Len had an appetite a dog would envy. Not like me and I know it bothered her. She watched me debating over my first choice. My wrists protruding from winceyette pyjama sleeves were stick thin. Another bout of Brucellosis had kept me shivering in my bed for the last week, and I know she despaired of my ever eating a full meal.

Len reached over for his second biscuit, but mother tapped him on the head. 'Wait your turn,' she snapped.

'Come on scraggy-Lil,' Len shoved at my elbow. 'Hurry up.'

'I'm not d'cided yet,' I replied. My hand wandered yet again between the bourbon and the wafer.

'Well decide and give the rest've us a chance,' said Len, mentally measuring the distance between himself and his mother in case another slap was heading his way.

Mother frowned, and gave him another sharp command of 'Wait.'

I grabbed at a wafer and a split second later dropped it as I snapped up the bourbon.

'Muuuum,' Len wailed. 'She touched that one. Tell her!'

'Susan,' my mother took the wafer and placed it firmly in front of me. 'That's your two.'

'But I wanted that one,' I said and snatched up an iced angel.

'She's got three now,' Len cried, and grabbed at the box. 'I'm having three as well.' Len grasped the tin's edge and scooped a second chocolate biscuit.

I grabbed my side of the tin and heaved on it, my arm whipped back as Len's grasp was broken and swept my mug across the table.

'Watch out for the... Oh God's'trewth,' Mother exclaimed

as a flood of steaming cocoa spread across the table top. She grabbed up a tea cloth and started mopping frantically. 'Bed. Now!' she shouted. 'Both of you.'

I sat watching the dark brown river flowing off the table top and felt my bottom lip began to quiver. 'My cocoa,' I whispered, and then louder, 'my cocoa! I'll get you for that, Len Birch.' I hurled the biscuits and then lunged at him.

Bo darted forward to snatch up this unexpected treat, and then turned to lick up the dribbling chocolate waterfall.

My father hustled Len into the front room and yanked me up from the chair, hugging me tightly, both to stem the tears and prevent me from launching another assault.

A sharp rap at the door caught everyone's attention; we froze in mid turmoil, and barely had time to turn around before the door opened.

'Good evening Birch,' the Guv'nor said. 'Mrs Birch.' He held out a large, plucked turkey with both hands.

Bo growled a deep rumbling warning that set his fur ruff trembling; then he caught the whiff of fresh meat. Guard duty forgotten his plumed tail began to wag frantically. He rose onto his hind legs; jaws closing rapidly around the gobbler's dangling head. The Guv'nor stepped back, and the dog's white teeth snapped loudly against thin air.

My father whistled sharply, and the dog shot under the table. An ugly silence descended on the room, yet the Guv'nor smiled calmly, as if he noticed nothing untoward. He proffered my mother the bird.

'Even'n, Sir,' she said finally. Wiping her hands on her apron, she grappled the huge turkey from him. It was enormous, probably twenty-five pounds and I could see from her dismayed expression that she was wondering how it would ever fit into the oven. At a loss, she bobbed a vestigial curtsey, embarrassed into pre-war habits of domestic service. 'Thank you, Sir. I'm sorry about the mess, Sir,' she stammered, 'but wel…'

'Busy time,' the Guv'nor said equably. He smiled at me.

'Good evening young lady. No hello today?'

''Lo,' I whispered. 'Sir,' I added as my father squeezed my arm gently.

The Guv'nor nodded and beckoned his daughter into the room. 'Close the door Mary-Anne,' he said. 'Don't let the cold in or Mrs Birch will never get her stove hot enough to get supper cooked.'

Mary-Anne sidled in, wary of the strained atmosphere and deposited two wrapped bottles and a tin of shortbread on the only un-cocoa-ed section of table available. Then she caught sight of the front room. 'Oh Daddy! Do come and look.' She rushed through the door and stood gaping at the ceiling. Len jumped to his feet as she entered and backed against the wall. She whirled in slow circles, staring at the gaudy array. 'Daddy, this is simply wonderful. Just like a fairy grotto. And look, the Christmas tree. It's so beautiful. Can we have some like this?'

The Guv'nor came to look at the swathes of colour festooned across the ceiling and walls, and shook his head in tolerant disbelief. 'I'm not sure that your mother would see it quite that way.' He glanced at my father and grinned. 'Though it is colourful I will say that. Maybe you could hang some in the nursery?'

'Could I? Oh goody.' She beamed at all and sundry, clapping her hands and looking far younger than her sixteen years.

'Do I detect young Susan's hand here?' the Guv'nor asked my father.

'Well ... Susan's been poorly again,' my father said. 'It keeps her occupied.'

The Guv'nor laughed, and my father relaxed in the shared joke. The Guv'nor was an ex-military man, and valued hard work and enthusiasm. His lady wife, however, the daughter of a Lord, would never tolerate homemade decorations in her home. Christmas in the 'Big House' arrived in a Harrods's van.

The Guv'nor smiled and patted my head. 'Yes, of course. Cook said you'd been unwell. My wife sent this for you.' He pulled a flat package from the front of his coat. 'Happy Christmas,' he told me.

I took the package shyly. 'Thank you,' I whispered eyes wide. 'Sir.'

'Well, Birch, I'll be on my way.' The Guv'nor motioned Mary-Anne toward the door. 'Happy Christmas all,' he said.

A chorus of 'Happy Christmas, Sir. Happy Christmas, Miss Mary-Anne,' followed them into the dark night.

When the door had closed and the sounds of the Land-Rover had faded, my parents turned to each other and sighed relief. Len beat a rapid retreat back to the train-set. Tears forgotten I went to sit beneath the Christmas tree with my mystery package. I glanced toward the kitchen to make sure I was not being observed before tearing a tiny hole in the edge of the paper and peeking inside. *Little Women*. My pulse quickened. A brand new book all for my very own. I peered in the tiny tear at the glossy colour cover.

A noise from the kitchen made me shove the package quickly under the tree. Tomorrow I would read it. After all, it was Christmas.

Granny Southam's Cake

1 lb butter

1½ lb flour

1 teaspoon mixed spice

1 teaspoon ground cinnamon

½ teaspoon ground nutmeg

½ teaspoon ground ginger

1 lb dark brown sugar

3 lb dried fruit (sultanas, raisins, currants, plus others if preferred, eg dates, figs)

4 oz cut peel (finely chopped)

4 oz glace cherries (roughly chopped)

4 oz blanched almonds (roughly chopped)

2 tablespoons honey or black treacle

9 eggs

Juice of 1 lemon

½ teaspoon vanilla essence

1 large glass of brandy

Method (make before Advent to allow it to mature)

1. At least one week before baking put the fruit in a large screw top jar and add brandy.

2. Turn the jar daily until brandy is soaked in (add more brandy if required)

3. Cream sugar and butter thoroughly

4. Add eggs and flour alternately.

5.   Stir in the rest of the ingredients.

6.   Add a little milk (or brandy!) if needed to make a stiff dropping consistency.

7.   Line a large cake tin with greased paper.

8.   Tie brown paper around the outside of the tin.

9.   Place salt in a roasting tin (about one inch) and stand the cake tin on the top.

10.   Preheat the oven to gas mark one or two, and place the cake in the centre of the oven.

11.   Bake for six to seven hours, or until a skewer comes away clean.

12.   Leave in the tin until cool.

13.   Remove the paper and trim the cake of any burned edges.

14.   Prick the top and sprinkle with brandy.

15.   Wrap the cake in greaseproof paper and store in a tin until mid December. (You can unwrap it in between times to add more brandy if desired.)

16.   Unwrap the cake, trim if required to get a smooth shape.

17.   Melt apricot jam and brush onto the cake.

18.   Roll out and cut marzipan to shape to cover all of the cake (or top only if preferred).

19.   When the marzipan is dry decorate with royal icing.

20.   This is a very large cake and you may want to divide the mix and make two. It is very rich, but keeps well.

21.   Try eating this Northern Counties style with a slice of sharp cheese and a wee dram.

Granny Hopcraft's Puds

3 lb mixed sultanas, raisins and other died fruits of choice (not currants: long cooking makes them gritty)

1lb dry suet (beef or vegetarian – both work equally well)

8 oz breadcrumbs

8 oz plain flour

4 oz almonds

4 oz glace cherries

1 oz candied peel

½ teaspoon salt

8 eggs

1 bottle of old ale (or barley wine if you cannot get old ale)

2 glasses of brandy

Sugar or honey (optional according to your taste; the mix is already sweet and seldom needs any extra)

Method (make before Advent)

1. Soak fruit in brandy for five days before cooking.

2. Mix all of the ingredients.

3. Spoon into pudding bowls to within a quarter inch of the top (makes average of two large or three small puddings).

4. Cover with greaseproof paper (or foil) and with a pudding cloth.

5. Tie on firmly, leaving a fold on both paper and cloth to allow the mixture to rise.

6. Boil for nine hours.

7. Remove cloth and paper and allow to go cold.

8. Recover with paper and cloth and store in a cool, dry place until Christmas.

9. Before use boil for at least one hour.

10. To be really festive and traditional you can add silver charms to the mixture but it is advisable to wrap them in a little greaseproof paper first [a] for hygiene, and [b] to prevent them being swallowed by mistake. At one time silver sixpences or threepenny bits (or joeys) would have been used; remember that modern coins do not have the same silver content, I would not advice using currency.

11. If you want to bring your pudding to the table flaming with brandy remember to warm the brandy gently first so that it is the brandy that burns – not your pud!

12. Serve with double cream, vanilla custard or brandy sauce (or all three if you're not worried about your waistline.)

Medicinal/Traditional

I am not sure whether you could claim any curative properties for cakes and puddings, except as a tonic for the spirit, but a curse for the waistline.

It is traditional for each person in the household to make a secret wish for the coming year as they take a turn in stirring the mix.

The traditional date for mixing your puddings is the last Sunday *before* Advent. A rhyme chanted for by children to remind mother of this was:

> *Stir up, we beseech thee*
> *the Pudding in the Pot,*
> *And when we get home,*
> *We'll eat it all hot.*

There are, of course, myriad details attached to the Yuletide plants and trees such as fir, holly, ivy and mistletoe. Here are just a few of them – *caution* these are not user friendly plants for medicinal use, *do not* take berries of any of these plants internally.

Medicinal – Fir

The smell of pine was supposed to cure all manner of ailments, especially those of the lungs.

Medicinal – Holly

A cure for chilblains was to 'thrash' them with holly twigs until they bled.

Powdered holly berries mixed with lard was a less drastic alternative.

Infants could be cured of all manner of things, including ruptures by being passed through a hole in a live holly tree.

New milk drunk from a variegated-holly cup would cure whooping cough

Holly berries were used often in animal medicine.

Note: holly berries can be toxic

Medicinal – Ivy

The whooping cough cure was also said to work from an ivy-wood bowl

Ivy soaked in vinegar was a cure for corns.

Wearing an ivy wreath prevented hair loss.

Ivy (good dark green ones) can by boiled in lard. The resultant ointment is a cure for burns and scalds. The same ointment cured scalp blemishes such as cradlecap.

Chop ivy leaves and boil them. The juice can be used to clean clothes such as serge and tweed, saving you dry cleaning bills!

Note: ivy berries are toxic.

Mistletoe

Mistletoe grown on hawthorn made into tea to cure for measles and whooping cough.

Berries dipped in male urine were said to cure jaundice.

Mistletoe broth will cure adenoid problems.

A bag of berries tied around an infant's neck will cure many 'childish' complaints.

Stems will reduce blood pressure, slow heart rate and slow tumour growth.

Also stems as a tincture for hardened arteries.

Note: mistletoe berries are toxic.

Traditional – Fir

The Christmas tree is a symbol of Yule or Christmas that almost anyone who has spent a December in Britain would recognise, and is basically a Teutonic custom brought to England by Queen Victoria's husband, Prince Albert. It has now been adopted worldwide.

The trimming of trees, however, is not unique to Prince Albert's birthplace. An early custom was a wish tree, which could be fir, though more usually was a birch branch. The tree would be placed bare in a strategic place and family and visitors would be invited to decorate it with ribbons or other trimmings as they made wishes. A wish tree was usually kept in the house from Winter Solstice until the festival of Imbolc (Candlemas Day).

It is said that to plant a row of firs would mean a loss of property – which could possibly explain the warring-neighbours phenomenon that seem to accompany the planting of cypresses.

Traditional – Holly

It was unlucky to bring holly into the house at any time other than for Yule, which is why, traditionally, Christmas decorations all went up on Christmas Eve (or Winter Solstice), and came down again on the Twelfth Night after that day.

It was not good luck to burn holly used in the decorations on the house fire, nor to throw it on a refuse heap.

Holly, especially one that is self-sown, is good protection from evil.

A holly-collar protected horses, hence many carters and drivers preferred holly-handles whips and chariot shafts were often made of holly.

Holly sticks brought back straying cattle: a holly walking stick would protect travellers.

Lightening is said never to strike a holly tree.

It is said to be very bad luck to cut down a holly tree, which is why until the recent habit of using mechanical hedge trimmers, hedgerows where often sprinkled with holly trees left by labourers to grow freely.

It is said that a heavy crop of berries foretells of a hard winter ahead.

Bird-lime was made boiling one part holly-bark juice with three parts nut oil.

Traditional – Ivy

Ivy was sacred to Dionysus and Bacchus and hung outside vintner's shops. It was also said that ivy strung across the path of a drunk would bring them to sobriety.

Ivy is said to be a feminine plant, yet many 'bad luck' tales tell that ivy should not go near hearth of cooking fire. Yet in some areas the last sheaf of the harvest home was 'Ivy Girl' twined with ivy strands and ribbons. It was often given to the tardiest farmer as an ironical comment.

Traditional – Mistletoe

Probably best known as the plant that allows kisses. Only mistletoe with berries should be used for a kissing bower, and a berry should be forfeited for every kiss.

Mistletoe used in a kissing wreath should not be discarded until the next Christmas.

Druids regard mistletoe (the Golden Bough) as their most sacred plant, harvesting it with gold sickles, letting the sprigs fall into a white cloth.

The mistletoe grown on oaks is the most prized, the berries being regarded as the Oak God's semen.

Mistletoe has traditionally been singled out to be banned from churches for its Druid connections – which is odd when holly, ivy and fir have almost as much clout in Pagan circles.

Glossary

Sussex Dialect Words and Phrases

Ampery: in poor health

Athirt: across

Bangs: brucellosis

Bait: snack eaten out in the fields or barns

Biddy bit: small amount

Buck rat: fully grown male rat

Bwoy: boy; a general term of greeting/acknowledgement.

Catched hot: caught a fever

Chee(s): roosting sites

Close: farmyard

Coombe: downland valley

Cullers: animals marked to be culled at next market day

Downs: hills, specifically South Downs, which stretch from
  Eastbourne to Winchester

Dunch: simpleton, idiot

Dup: walk very quickly

En: catch-all for it, that, those, him, her, you, them, they, etc.

Farisees (sometimes written as Pharisees): fairies

Frith: young underwood/ undergrowth, specifically that growing by/
  under hedges, or edges of woodland.

Hatchety: tetchy

Hob: male ferret

Gabardine mac: ubiquitous school uniform coat from 1920s to late 1960s: double-breasted, belted coat, usually with detachable hood. (From personal experience, seldom as waterproof as the term 'mac' might imply.)

Gaffer: grandfather; boss man

Gobbler: turkey

Goody: title given to an elderly widow. Possibly refers to Goodening, the door to door alms collecting by the needy widows of the parish on St Thomas Day.

Gratten: stubble field (stubble being cut stems of corn still rooted in the earth)

Gurt: large, big

Guvnor: boss

Knucker: water dragon of Sussex folklore

Lapsy: lazy

Maid: general greeting/ acknowledgement for young woman/ girl

Mag-weed: may weed or *Anthemis cotula,* a form of chamomile – a common skin-irritant

Mews: seagulls

Musses: general greeting/ acknowledgement for married woman

Mus Reynolds: Mr Fox.

Old jack: farm-made scrumpy cider

Ore: seaweed washed up by the tide

Paigles: cowslips

Parz'mut: parsnip

Punkie Night: traditional Sussex celebration on all-hallows night

Robbutt: rabbit

Scaddle: to play truant

Screws: rheumatism etc.

Shaw: small wood, esp. one that shelters a farmyard or building

Shearlings: ewes in their first lambing

Sheer-way: bridle path/unmade road

Sheer-meeces: field mice

Shrammed: to be shivering with cold

Sock lamb: one raised by hand

Splash: shallow pond for soaking cart wheels (to prevent wood shrinkage).

Starved o' cold: to perish from the cold

Swop and bill hooks: hedging tools

Tersn't: isn't

Tilth: soil dug and raked to a fine consistency without clumps or rocks

Tis babs fer en: that's children for you

Whapple-way: bridle path through woods or fields

Wetting rod: long hand-held sharpening stone

Windshaken: thin and/ or puny animal

Withies: willows, specifically beds of young willow growth

Worritin: worrying or fussing over people or happenings

Wrap-over-pinny: cover-all apron, which is wrapped across the front and fastened with a small tie

Wurzel: mangold wurzel, a large beet crop usually grown for winter animal feed.

Yaffler: woodpecker; often used to denote a foolish or idiotic person

Yowe: ewe

Yoystering: playing the noisily – to be rowdy

34093350R00120

Made in the USA
Charleston, SC
30 September 2014